RAVEN REACHED FURTHER INTO THE NET AND
DREW MORE OF IT TOWARD HER.

> I am Raven—I rule here—identify
yourself <

With a roar the cloud engulfed her and
all the lights went out. Around her the darkness beat against her, leaving her defenseless before a rage that was like a force of
nature.

> RAVEN RAVEN RAVEN RAVEN RAVEN
RAVEN RAVEN RAVEN RAVEN RAVEN RAVEN
RAVEN RAVEN RAVEN RAVEN RAVEN RAVEN . . .
<

Her own name beat against her brain
over and over again. The cloud buffeted her
with the power of its fury; throwing images
of darkness, death and pain at her until she
screamed with the sensory overload. She
flew for the edge of blackness but she was
dragged back into the whirling eye of the
hurricane. It was trying to break her and the
moment she realized that she let go, shutting out everything.

Now she stood, completely alone, staring at the computer screen. Something
inside the net hated her and it would stop at
nothing to destroy her. Even if that meant
destroying the next in the process.

Hex by Rhiannon Lassiter

Hex

Hex: Shadows

Hex: Ghosts

Available from Simon Pulse

GHOSTS

Rhiannon Lassiter

SIMON PULSE

NEW YORK   LONDON   TORONTO   SYDNEY   SINGAPORE

First Simon Pulse edition June 2002

Text copyright © 2000 by Rhiannon Lassiter

SIMON PULSE
An imprint of Simon & Schuster
Children's Publishing Division
1230 Avenue of the Americas
New York, NY 10020

Designed by O'Lanso Gabbidon
The text of this book was set in Palatino.
Printed in the United States of America
2 4 6 8 10 9 7 5 3 1

Library of Congress Control Number available from the
Library of Congress.

ISBN 0-7434-2213-9

Dedicated to my family:
Stephen, Marushka, Rebecca, and Jessica.
Also to Sara and Sophie for lending me books.

Contents

Introduction

In the late 21st century, genetics experiments led to mutations in the population and the creation of a new breed of people known as Hexes. Feared for their ability to interface with technology, the Hexes were declared a threat to international security and across the world governments sanctioned their legalized extermination.

But the European Federation, the most tyrannical and repressive of the world governments, secretly authorized an illegal laboratory dedicated to performing experiments in the hope that the dangerous Hex abilities could be utilized or at least understood. In this facility thousands of children, unfortunate enough to possess the Hex gene, were experimented on, tortured and murdered.

In the year 2367 a Hex named Raven attempted to make the existence of this laboratory public, only to have it destroyed and the records hidden by agents of the English government and the European

Federation. Raven, with her brother Wraith, and their companions Ali, Kez and Luciel went into hiding.

In 2369 Dr. Kalden, the scientist in charge of the illegal laboratory, captured Raven and attempted to restart the experiments. The other members of her group, with the help of an anti-EF organization called Anglecynn, rescued Raven and began working in earnest to bring down the corrupt European government.

Two years on, the Federation have not managed to find the Hexes despite the best efforts of the CPS, their brutal enforcers. But Raven and her associates have staked out abandoned areas of the sprawling city of London and continue to work in secret for the day when they can be safe.

1

Tried in the Fire

Drow dropped off the edge of the walkway, landing with a jolt that knocked the breath out of his body. A blaster shot zinged past his head and he didn't waste time on catching his breath, staggering to his feet and running to where the arches sloped down to a lower level. He heard more shots around him but the Seccies were falling behind. A street kid wasn't worth the trouble of an extended chase and he was heading into the depths of the ganglands now.

The lighting on the next level was damaged, flickering erratically and creating odd shadows against the skyscraper sections emblazoned with gang colors. This was Spider territory: not far from home, but Drow kept to the shadows anyway. The Spiders wouldn't cause him hassle as long as he didn't mess with them; it was their style. Their territory was the rec complexes that surrounded Drow now: vice-joints, dream palaces and gaming 'cades. They catered to the low-wagers who couldn't afford to move up to the heights of the city but could spare the creds for a cheap thrill. The locals paid protection money to the Spiders and the gang patrolled the streets but, while they would get tough if they needed to, they didn't waste their time shaking down anyone wearing the wrong colors.

Drow weaved his way through Spider town, checking back over his shoulder casually every once in a while. As far as he could tell, the Seccies had cut their losses and decided not to follow him into the ganglands. But that didn't mean he was safe. They had holocams on their flitter and a record of him running away. If they picked him up later they'd be able to ID him as the kid who'd stolen a case of data discs from the Fractured Image. For now though he was as chill as you could be on the streets. Heading down through the levels of Spider territory he mapped out the route ahead in his mind. He had two choices and neither gave him much of a buzz. The way back home to his own gang's sector lay through Katana space. The knife gang wouldn't like his colors and if they caught him short-cutting through their turf he might not only lose the discs he'd lifted but wake up dead tomorrow. The alternative would take longer, circling Katana territory through the Ghost area. However, the Katanas were a menace Drow understood: no one knew anything about the Ghosts.

Catching sight of his own reflection in the grimy windows of a black-market tech store, Drow made up his mind. The fragments of shining circuitry braided into his black hair and the silvery mirror lenses in his eyes marked him as a Chrome, and a lone ganger was a target on the streets. The Katanas were expanding their area and any stranger would be fair game to enhance their rep. The Ghosts were known to be hard as ice and no one gave them trouble but they were a secretive gang and didn't need to prove themselves all the time. They controlled levels and enclaves all over the skyrises and starscrapers of London but never displayed their colors or openly hung out on the street. Ghost territory was a no-go area and gangs who tangled with them suffered runs of bad luck that made them suspicious of the Ghosts and wary of trouble. Standing in line for a public grav-tube to the levels lower down, Drow tried not to remember the other stories he had heard about the Ghosts. It was rumored they stole children to increase their numbers and that they were anarchists trying to bring down the city through terrorist action. It had been reported on the holovid that the Ghosts were linked to Anglecynn: a terrorist faction that engineered net crashes and gang attacks on European Federation agencies. But whenever the Seccies made a move on Ghost enclaves they arrived to find everything abandoned, not even trash left behind. Meanwhile, the Ghosts started up in some other wasted section of the city ganglands and the local gang steered clear.

The other people waiting for the grav-tube gave Drow sidelong looks. Two kids wearing Spider colors, at about thirteen just a couple of years younger than him, gave him lazy salutes. Trying to act it up like they were real hard men but chill enough not to try and prove it, Drow thought. The rest of the tube-riders were mostly low-wagers: looking at Drow shiftily until they dismissed him as too young to be a threat. That wasn't true, any street kid had to be able to take care of themselves, but Chromes didn't fight for thrills and Drow ignored the looks. The grav-tube car arrived with a low hiss and Drow dropped a three cred piece into the slot, receiving a piece of scrip for three levels down in return. Behind him the line shuffled along and the car filled quickly with people. Just before it took off another two people hurried aboard and Drow blinked in momentary surprise. The boy didn't look to be much older than Drow but he held himself with a self-assurance that made him seem much more experienced. Drow felt certain the stranger was a ganger, although he wore no symbols or colors on his clothes. But it was the girl who really drew his attention. There was no way a girl like that could be a ganger. She wore white, an unusual color down in the slums since it attracted notice and was quickly stained by the grimy streets, and her shining pale blonde hair and graceful stance made her look even more out of place. Drow couldn't take his eyes off her as the grav-car sank down through the levels and it was with a jolt that he realized that they had reached his destination and both the strangers were disembarking ahead of him.

Drow stumbled off the grav-car and on to the level. The strangers were already some distance ahead of him but Drow forgot about them when he noticed the silence of the streets. No other gang territory was ever this deserted. All the skyscraper sections on this level were shuttered up but they didn't look abandoned so much as closed off. Garbage and debris littered the streets but the areas in front of the buildings were swept clean and the doors were sturdy enough to be blast-proof. Glancing around warily, Drow realized that some buildings were empty, doors and windows damaged or gone. Those empty doorways worried him. Anyone could be hiding within: sentries watching for intruders into Ghost territory. Drow only hoped that he looked unthreatening enough for them to leave him alone. That thought suddenly reminded him of the couple ahead and he lengthened his stride to catch up a little, trying to keep them in sight. The girl's long white coat flapped in the still air behind her and the boy's hair glinted bronze under the streetlights. No sunlight filtered this far into the depths but Drow found the artificial lighting eerie. Despite the emptiness of the level the Ghosts obviously chose to keep the lights working. Instinctively, Drow scanned the area for holocams: the Seccies had them placed all over the upper levels to keep an eye on people. At first he could see nothing, but then a small black box on the side of a building caught his attention. Beside it someone had scrawled a graffiti image of a black bird with outspread wings. Across the street and lower down there was another slightly differently shaped box with the same bird emblem next to it. Drow's heart rate began to speed up as his eyes flickered

across the scene. Black birds seemed to leap
out at him from all directions and he realized that, if each symbol meant some kind
of surveillance tech, he was under more
complete observation than when he ven-
tured into the Seccie-patrolled upper levels
of the city. He checked ahead for the figures
of the two strangers but they had crossed
the plaza ahead and rounded the corner of a
building. Drow followed their route cautiously just in case there was an ambush
ahead. But when he got to the spot where
they'd disappeared there was nothing. Not
a sound stirred across the level, although in
the distance he could hear the thrum of
activity above and below. The strangers
must have been Ghosts, Drow realized
uncomfortably, and he was lucky they
hadn't taken exception to his presence in
their area. With that in mind he picked up
his speed and kept to a smooth run across
the level, heading as fast as he could back to
Chrome territory.

As the door slid closed behind them Ali
frowned to herself and then glanced at Kez.
"Was he following us?" she asked.
"Don't think so," Kez replied. "But let's
check." He touched the keypad on his
wrist-com lightly while Ali waited. They

were standing in the foyer on one of the larger building sections that their group claimed and, in contrast to the deserted streets outside, the large room was a hive of activity. A flitter was parked in the middle of the space and three gangers in blue and gold Snake colors were unloading crates of equipment. Over to one side a larger group of Anglecynn members were going through a final weapons check and Geraint, their leader, flipped Ali a brief wave when he noticed her. The Ghosts were an unusual allegiance of different groups and in the two years they had spent hiding from the Seccies the gang had grown hugely. Ali had begun to like the feeling of being an important part of the group and she found herself smiling as she looked around the room.

Even more reassuring was the feeling of safety that came from being part of a large group. Despite their attacks on the brutal laws of the European Federation, no member of the group had been captured. The Hexes used their ability to interface with the net to gain information that the group could use. Their consistent attacks on EF facilities and their release of restricted information made it increasingly difficult for the government to cover up how much the regime was hated. Most important to Ali were the young Hexes they had successfully rescued from extermination. Despite the Civil Protection Service's best efforts to keep their records secret, the Hex group found them and tried to get to the victims before the CPS could. To some of these children their Hex abilities came as a complete surprise but to others who, like Ali, had lived in fear of discovery for almost all their lives, the Ghosts were the first real Ghosts because they aimed to be uncatchable and because none of them had any legal identity. They took their safety seriously and even minor threats, like the ganger boy who had followed them down to Ghost territory, were responded to quickly and efficiently.

Kez had stopped speaking into his wrist-com and Ali looked at him inquiringly.

"Jordan's reviewing the surveillance holos but she thought the kid was just taking a shortcut," Kez explained. "I don't think we have a problem."

"In that case we'd better get going," Ali replied. "There's a briefing in an hour's time, we have two rescue attempts tomorrow and Alaric's team have a plan to sabotage Seccie communications."

"Electric!" Kez grinned, and as Ali smiled back she realized he was enjoying life as much as she was. Two years ago they'd disliked each other; Kez resenting her for her privileged upbringing and she despising him for growing up on the streets. But now the group was so much larger the differences between them no longer seemed important and there was always too much work to do to waste time quarreling.

As they headed up through the building, friends and allies greeting them briefly as they went about their work, Ali thought about the rescued children who were the main focus of her own activities in the group. There were almost two hundred of them now, ranging in age from five to as old as Ali herself. It was Raven's responsibility to teach them to use their Hex abilities but Ali, Kez and Luciel were responsible for the rest of their education and for any other needs they might have. It was demanding work. Wraith and Raven virtually ran the Ghosts and one of the few things they agreed on was that the Hex children should grow up with every possible advantage the group could provide. As a result Ali was having to relearn things she'd never paid any attention to at school in the luxurious Belgravia complex just to stay one step ahead of her students. Kez soaked up knowledge like a sponge, Luciel experimented constantly with new teaching methods and ideas and between the three of them they had constructed an education course that covered everything from philosophy to firearms. Their reward was that the children liked and trusted them, although they were still wary around Raven.

The thought of the group's leader caused a shadow to pass over Ali's cheerful mood. The children weren't the only ones to have been trained by Raven: the older Hexes relied on her to give them the benefit of her experience. Luciel had progressed by leaps and bounds; his ambition to be a scientist had been revived by what Raven taught him of his abilities and he was trying to write a study explaining them. Avalon, the former rock singer, had successfully integrated her powers into her music and was still entranced by the idea of being a Hex. Although she remained on the sidelines of the group, her celebrity continued to gain the Hex cause prominence in the media. But Ali, despite her best efforts to understand Raven's teaching, was intimidated by the net. She had progressed sufficiently in her studies that she could wander happily through databases and nodes. But secured systems alarmed her and the infinite depths of the data network made her feel scared. She sometimes wondered if Raven was more like the net than a human being. The dark-eyed Hex with her cold summaries of people and the situations and her dizzying mood swings reminded Ali of the dark, unknown expanses of information which frightened her.

The flitter hung like a bird above the city and Raven stared down at her domain. She came here more and more often now, watching the starscrapers linked by a glittering network of bridges and arches sinking into bottomless depths where no light penetrated. Up here she felt like a Ghost, unseen and intangible, with the cityscape spread out beneath her like an array of complex circuitry. While the others had found fulfillment in being part of a group, Raven felt increasingly stifled. None of them was any match for her, in abilities or imagination, and as she trained the legion of Hex children she wished that just once they would find in a Hex who had struggled as she had had to and triumphed.

"What are you thinking?" a voice asked quietly and Raven turned to regard her companion. Cloud Estavisit was the least likely member of their group. Cloud had fallen from the pinnacle of fame with Avalon and had tried to save them both by betraying the Hexes. He'd made up for his treachery when he'd saved their lives, but most of the Ghosts still felt uncomfortable around him. However, Raven saw in him a foil for her own black moods and a companion in her isolation.

"That maybe Kalden was right," she said softly.

"Kalden?" Cloud raised an eyebrow. "The scientist who experimented on all those children? I thought he was supposed to be renowned for his evil."

"To simply say something is evil means you refuse to understand it," Raven replied, turning to look back down into the maze of the city. "Research like Kalden's cannot be dismissed, no matter how twisted its origins."

"So why was he right?"

"For the wrong reasons," Raven replied. "He was trying to exterminate the Hexes but the trauma he subjected them to unleashed their potential in a way my training hasn't been able to duplicate." She swore suddenly under her breath, her fists clenching with frustration. "We just don't have the knowledge," she hissed. "There's so much we don't understand and I can't even teach all I know."

"Are you advocating torture as part of the training program?" Cloud asked ironically. "I can't see Wraith liking that option much."

"No, I'm not advocating it." Raven's

voice was drained and lifeless. "But it was being forced to struggle that made me what I am and so far I am unique."

"Poor Raven." Cloud laughed mockingly. "Only godlike powers and the European Federation living in fear of you. What more does life have to offer?"

Raven grinned, her mood changing suddenly at Cloud's irreverence, and her dark eyes flashed.

"Damned if I know," she said. "Come on, let's fly."

Smiling back, Cloud touched the controls lightly and the flitter fell like a hawk toward London.

Night was falling across Europe but in the glittering splendor of Versailles it brought anything but peace. Sergei Sanatos, the Federation President, scanned the ranks of his advisers with barely hidden fury. The most powerful men in Europe struggled to maintain their equanimity in the face of his rage.

"Sir President," the Governor of the CPS began cautiously. "We have taken all possible precautions—"

"Enough!" Sergei slammed his fist down on the table with a crash that made all the advisers jump. "You speak of possibilities and precautions. I want facts. I want this rogue Hex caught and for the past two years you've failed to give her to me!"

Charles Alverstead took a deep breath. He wanted Raven caught almost as badly as the President did. It had been during his governorship that she'd escaped from them, despite security measures he had personally approved. He'd been able to blame her escape on Kalden, the scientist studying her, but now he was running out of excuses.

"The situation is difficult," he began again. "England was one of the last countries to be brought under EF rule and our attempts to tighten up security there have caused deep resentment. It seems the Hexes have formed some sort of alliance with an established terrorist group, and despite sending Federation troops to work with the Security Services we have no way of combating an enemy who knows our every move in advance."

"We've tried keeping records off the net," the Minister of Internal Affairs added. "But our system would collapse if we attempted it on a large scale. We can't control the Federation without instantaneous data transfer. Information is the currency in which large governments deal. We've worked for years to prevent a Hex from gaining power over the net because without it we are crippled."

"I know we are crippled," Sergei said softly and dangerously. "Your continued failure to deliver this Hex tells me that much at least."

"Sir President, we will capture her," Alverstead said quickly. "There have been threats to international security before and we've overcome them. There were other mutants before this—"

"Wait!" Sergei held up a hand and Alverstead stopped speaking as the President's cold gray eyes narrowed in thought. "There have been threats before this," the President mused. "How did we combat them?"

"Those events occurred during your predecessor's rule and the information is classified, Sir," the Minister for Internal Affairs began but as Sergei's expression grew dangerous he added: "But doubtless we can find it."

"Does no one know anything?" the President snapped in annoyance and around the table the senior ministers shook their heads.

"Sir President?" a measured voice spoke up and they all turned to regard the elderly Minister of Propaganda, the man who controlled all European communications and media agencies. He was nodding to himself, a slight smile playing across his wrinkled lips. "The events you speak of are known to me. It was my department that handled the subsequent cover-up. The Federation was threatened by a mutant once before, twenty-five years ago. Listen and I will tell you how it happened. . . ."

The cloak of the night fell over England and France like velvet wings and moved to capture the rest of Europe in its darkness. South and east of the palace of Versailles, night touched another palace where water lapped through the once splendid hallways and the crumbling wrecks of other ornate mansions surrendered to the inevitable triumph of the sea. From the top of the golden stone palace Tally looked out across the grand canal and gazed on the ruin that was once Venice in the last rays of the dying sun.

It was the only home she had ever known, although most of her life had been spent fleeing from one country to another. It was to Venice that her mother had brought them, exhausted by the chase and looking only for safety and silence. While their mother had tried to make a home for them in the ruined palazzo, Tally and her twin brother had discovered the forgotten history of Europe, explored the art galleries and museums with their treasure-trove of ruined beauty and moored their boat to the pinnacle of St. Mark's Cathedral while they watched the sun set over the island city the sea had reclaimed. Now their mother was dying and Tally couldn't see the magic of the city any longer. The life she had known was coming to an end and she was afraid to admit it even to herself.

These last few months Tally and Gift had immersed themselves in the past, but the romantic splendors of doomed Venice were as alien to the world of the twenty-fourth century as the life they had lived up to now. Amid the technological sophistication of EF-ruled Europe they had lived in the shadows of the system, camping in the wilderness abandoned or rejected by the technocracy and avoiding the vast data-hives of the urban megaplexes. Only briefly had they even seen cities—while being smuggled through and around them by allies or gangers bribed to assist them. Even in so precarious an existence, their mother had educated the children to the best of her ability, but Tally knew when her mother died it might be too late to learn the familiarity with the high-tech world that the city-dwellers took for granted.

Her brother's voice came floating up

from the floor below and Tally got reluctantly to her feet.

"Tally!" He was still calling her, his voice high and anxious. "Tally! Come quickly!"

"I'm here!" Tally broke into a run, jumping down through the hole in the broken roof to land on the floor below. Inside the palazzo darkness and dust seemed to cover everything. But in one of the once luxurious suites her brother had kindled a fire and the light was like a beacon as she made her way through the dark.

"There you are!" Her twin appeared suddenly from the shadows like a confused mirror image. Her own golden-brown eyes stared back at her from his face, framed by the same auburn hair. "I was scared you weren't coming back."

"Where would I go, Gift?" she asked. "There's nowhere left to run to."

"Then perhaps it's time to stop running," a weak voice said softly and Tally turned to face the bed where her mother lay.

Her name was Harmony and she had been a beautiful woman once. The rich auburn hair she had bequeathed to her children hung limply around her gaunt pale face and the same golden eyes watched them tenderly. But what she retained of her beauty was little enough. The years of fear had worn away at her and sapped her strength until she couldn't go on any longer.

"Mother," Tally said softly, her voice breaking. "How do you feel?"

"No worse, darling." Harmony tried to smile and lifted a thin arm toward her children. "Come here and kiss me."

The twins came to sit on her bed, each taking one of her hands, and Harmony again tried to smile, comforting them as best she could in the little time that remained to her.

"I must talk to you now before it's too late," she began. "There are things you need to know. . . ."

"His name was Theo Freedom and he was the danger we had always feared," the Minister for Propaganda explained. "Listen closely, for this is a story I had never thought I would need to tell. It begins with the greatest secret of all: of how and why the Hexes were created."

Around the table the assembled dignitaries leaned closer as the Propaganda Minister lowered his voice. Even the President looked around warily, although none knew better than he how safe the security was here at the political heart of the Federation. Past governments had shrouded the events of their rules in secrecy, as did the current administration, and none of them had any direct experience of the Hex threat. The object of their fear fascinated and repelled them as the old man related how a Hex might shake the Federation from its foundations.

"Our ancestors were misguided in their march toward progress. They experimented with genetics and created mutants intended to be a fusion of mind and machine, technological wizards who would guide us into a new age and some day out into the stars."

The Propaganda Minister snorted contemptuously.

"They were fools and dreamers and they thought to play God. It has taken centuries for us to undo their work. They released the Hex gene into the world, wanting to give everyone the 'benefits' of the mutation. They didn't think of the dangers. There is such a thing as too much knowledge. Our society is founded on privacy, there are secrets that must be kept hidden for the good of humanity."

The President of the Federation nodded and around the table there were murmurs of assent. All of these political leaders had secrets they wished to hide: abuses of power and privilege and petty injustices against the people they had been elected to serve.

"However, there were some who had doubts, who understood that the Hex gene was an abomination that never should have been allowed to exist and politicians campaigned strenuously to make the use of the Hex abilities illegal. Once those laws had been passed it was the next logical step to make the mutants themselves illegal, to deprive them of any standing in the Federation. And, of course, when they did not know how to use their abilities it was easy to hunt them down.

"I would not know this tale myself but twenty-five years ago what we feared came to pass. A mutant in full control of his abilities single-handedly waged war against the Federation. Theo Freedom was a scientist, a brilliant young researcher without the slightest suspicion of treason ever attached to him. He had the highest levels of security access and the best laboratory facilities the Federation could provide. We had hoped to use him to create a plague that would wipe out the Hexes forever. But we made a mistake.

"Theo was a Hex himself. A mutant clever enough to hide his true nature from everyone who knew him. For five years he studied the Hex gene and the Hex abilities and *taught himself how to use them.*"

The Propaganda Minister paused and looked significantly around the table. Charles Averstead, the head of the CPS, shuddered. Keeping the Hexes from ever understanding their abilities had been the purpose of the Federation government for generations. Now he feared that the elusive Raven, the Hex he had captured and lost, was as great a threat as Theo Freedom had ever been. He had seen Raven himself. She had seemed barely more than a child and her black eyes had regarded him with a cool disdain as if she had known even then she would escape him. If a child Hex could evade the forces of the Federation government for so long and incite rebellion against the government, what more could she achieve when she was an adult?

"We had no knowledge of this, of course," the Propaganda Minister was saying. "We found out too late that Theo had not only studied the Hex gene but had passed on the knowledge to his son, who also carried the mutation. When a suspicious lab assistant reported that Theo Freedom was using the laboratory to carry out unusual tests on himself and his family we sent a team to investigate. Theo was captured and interrogated but his son had disappeared and not even under torture would he confess the young man's whereabouts.

"More importantly," and here the Minister's creaky voice sank to a whisper, "Theo's research had also disappeared. Enough data to write a book about the Hexes was copied to disk the day his son vanished and neither it nor he have ever been located.

"There have been false leads and suspicions but the son was never captured. Our only hope is that he is dead and the information he carries lost forever. We have no way to combat an active Hex, and with Theo Freedom's research a Hex could destroy us."

"And so your grandfather gave the files to your father and when he sacrificed himself so that we could escape, your father gave them to me."

Harmony coughed raspingly and Tally hurriedly filled a glass of water and held it to her lips.

"Thank you," she whispered, after she had sipped a little of it and she tightened her grip on her children's hands. "I have never shared her abilities but I have held the files in trust for you so that some day you might learn to understand them. I never thought that we'd be running so long that there would be no time to even teach you the basics. I hoped we'd find some place safe where I could teach you how to use the knowledge the files contained. Your father named you in hope that eventually the Hex gene would be recognized, not as a mutation, but as something to be treasured: a Gift, a Talent . . ."

The twins looked at each other. Their mother's story had filled them with longing for the father they had barely known and the grandfather they had never met. Tally voiced both of their thoughts when she asked:

"But what should we *do* with them? Can we learn to use them on our own?"

"Perhaps you don't have to do it alone," her mother said softly. "Two years ago terrorists attacked the Federation. A Hex escaped from the Federation Consulate in England. Just as your grandfather did, Hexes are again trying to strike against the Federation and his knowledge will help them to succeed."

"Terrorists?" Tally asked dubiously but Gift interrupted her.

"We've been running from Federation troops all our lives," he said fiercely. "If this gives us a chance to strike back we should take it. We've never even used our abilities but the government would kill us if they knew what we are. If these other Hexes understand the files they can use them to protect all of us."

"I hope so," Harmony said quietly. "I wish I could keep you safe myself, my children. I don't want to leave you alone." Her eyes closed and an expression of pain crossed her face.

"We'll be all right, Mother," Tally said quickly, pretending a confidence she didn't feel to comfort her mother. "We know what we have to do." She looked at Gift for confirmation and he nodded.

"We'll make you proud," he assured. "Don't worry about us."

Tally turned to look at her twin. They were both on the brink of tears but neither of them cried. The journey ahead consumed too much of their thoughts. The road before them was long and dangerous and neither of them was sure how to begin.

2

Begotten of the Dead

Drow didn't arrive back in Chrome territory
until night had fallen. To a rival ganger the
lonely streets decorated with Chrome symbols and colors would have seemed threat-
ening but to him they were home and he felt
himself relaxing. After he'd made his way
through Ghost territory, mercifully unchal-
lenged by the mysterious gang, he'd almost
run into a Seccie patrol and he'd lain low
again, crouching in the shelter of the bridge
while skimmers hummed past, waiting for
the cover of night to bring him safely home.

Now he threaded his way through his
own streets, still carrying the disks he had
lifted, eager to show his haul to his family.
The route he was following brought him
into a wide plaza and two shadowy figures
stepped out in front of him. Drow tensed

but relaxed almost immediately. The two men wore Chrome colors and the silver threaded into their braids shone faintly in the flickering lighting.

"It's Drow," he said quickly and added the password. "Chrome untarnished."

"Drow!" One of the men moved forward into the light and Drow recognized Innuru, his sister's husband. "You've been gone too long. The family was concerned."

"I ran into some Seccie trouble," Drow explained, proud to look so calm about it in front of the older gangers. "I had to cut through Ghost turf to get back."

Innuru looked surprised for a moment, then he grinned.

"Brave boy," he said, putting an arm around Drow's shoulder. "Come home and tell us about it. Your sister was worried."

The other ganger disappeared back into the shadows and Innuru and Drow headed toward the building their family had claimed as a home. As they passed through the familiar passageway and heard the sound of music thumping from further inside the building Drow fumbled in his jacket for the disks. There were ten of them, carefully slotted into the plain black case marked with the logo of the Fractured Image datastore.

"Lifted some disks," Drow said casually.

"New programs straight off the rack: access programs and encryption algorithms for the net."

Now Innuru did look impressed and he whistled softly as he looked over the disks.

"Your father will be pleased—" he was saying as they entered the main room and the rest of his words were cut off as Electra instantly ran to take Drow in her arms.

As he assured his sister he was all right, Drow looked around the room. His family had obviously been worried. His father was looking up with a smile of relief from his work table, loaded as usual with half-finished circuitry, and his other sisters, Selver and Arachne, looked equally relieved.

"Drow had some problems with Seccies," Innuru said darkly and Drow's father scowled. "But he got us some disks with electric programs, pure gold dust."

As Electra released him, saying she would find him something to eat, Drow basked in the approval of his family as his father carefully unpacked the disk case and commented on the haul.

"You've a good eye," he said with a pleased expression. "You couldn't have picked a better selection. There are programs here that won't be on the net for weeks."

Drow's heart sang and he could barely

wait to connect to the net to see the programs in action. But Electra fussed over him relentlessly until he sat down and ate the dinner she dialed from the Nutromac unit. Electra watched him to stop him from bolting his food but he was still finished quickly and his father beckoned him to the row of computer terminals at the side of the room and handed him two of the disks.

"See what you can get out of these," he suggested. "But don't do too much tonight. We have plenty of time."

Drow barely heard him. The terminal drew him with an irresistible fascination. As his hands played the keypad like a musical instrument he could feel himself sinking into the trance-like state the net always caused in him. His father said he had a natural talent for hacking but Drow suspected it was more than that. He couldn't describe the feeling he had when he was connected but he imagined that flying must feel something like it. He soared with the net and it lifted and carried him through its endless data pathways.

The net hummed with life like a city and Drow sped along its familiar pathways. On his own he could only travel so far. The net seemed to multiply the deeper he wandered, every junction or turning offering a dazzling multiplicity of choices, but now the access program he carried with him navigated the virtual city and remembered the path he had taken, so that looking back he could see the route he had taken laid out as a silver vein through all the twists and turns of the moving datastreams. The network was a shining place this evening: a phantom city exuding light and life, in contrast to the shadows that lurked in the physical reality. But as Drow traveled its pathways he could feel shadows in the net as well. There had always been darkened places where access was restricted or the flow of information slowed. But tonight he could feel a darkness as a tangible presence clouding the edge of his perceptions. It hung around the edge of the network as the night did around London, fogging the edges of the furthest datastreams, swirling through the remotest nodes like a contagion and never settling anywhere for long.

Puzzled, Drow paused in his exploration. Then cautiously he extended his perceptions, feeling for the darkness. It lurked in the distance and, relaxing, Drow flew toward it. The sense of wrongness it gave him was his only guide as the moving flows of data buffeted him in different directions like air currents. Then, all of a sudden, he had fallen through space to the heart of the darkness and the life of the net seemed

lightyears away. Everything was dead here
and silent but he could feel the black fog, of
which he was now a part, reaching out tendrils to still the heartbeat of the city.

> where am I? < he wondered, not
expecting an answer. But his question rang
back to him from every direction like a tor-
mented echo unable to stop.

> where? where . . . ? where . . . ? am I?
where am I? where am I? am I am I am I
am? <

He tried to screen out the endless repetitions and eventually felt them dying away,
the words descending into meaninglessness
as they receded further and further into the
gloom. Confused he tried again, more carefully.

> what/where is this?—everything is
dark/dead/lifeless—why—? <

This time the echoes rang in his head
like a scream and he was no longer sure if
they even were echoes.

> darkness . . . darkness . . . where?
where? darkness . . . dark/dead/dark down
in the darkness of death . . . where . . .
w . . . h . . . e . . . r . . . e . . . ? we here? hear?
darkness . . . death . . . <

Drow pulled himself away. Somewhere
in the dark there was a glimmer of consciousness and as the echoes rang on and
on, the words melding with each other to

become a speechless wail of despair, a shiver crossed his mind. Someone else was here in the net with him and they were insane. The darkness was the shreds of their mind.

He steeled himself for another attempt at communication but then froze where he was, hanging in virtual space at the center of the cloud. It was searching for him, he could feel it. Tracing his position by the thought or echoes of thoughts he had set off. Without him to begin the pattern it could barely think, but like a giant amoeba searching for a brain it was hunting him with the words it had stolen from him.

> where? where? where? am I/you? I am? where???? <

Wrenching himself away, he threw his mind out of the dark wildly, spinning in all directions, thinking only to get away. Until his consciousness came to rest in a river of light; a vast datastream flowing through the electronic maze and soothing him with its murmuring data until he came to shore at a node he recognized and, half-dazed, found the current that carried him home.

Disengaging himself from the terminal, he shuddered and manually ordered the program to forget the location it had mapped for that dark cloud. Whatever it was, he wanted no part of it or its images of

darkness and death. Although he didn't
know what it was there was something he
was sure of. Darkness and death were parts
of its nature. It had fed on them and made
them part of itself. As he wiped the record
of the cloud from his terminal he wondered
with a shudder how such a thing had ever
penetrated the net.

It was late at night when Ali finally
stopped working. Wraith had been adamant
that the Hex children weren't to be housed
together, the way orphans had been in the
asylum blockhouse where he and Raven
had grown up. Each adult in the community had to take the responsibility of caring
for one of the children, he had said, and
despite some hitches the plan had worked
well. Some of the Ghosts didn't have the
time to spare to care for a child and Raven
had flatly refused. But others were prepared
to look after two or three and the result was
a thriving community of unconventional
family groups in which each child had at
least one "parent" to look after them. However, it meant that Ali, Kez and Luciel had
to make sure that every single one of them
was collected at the end of the day. Since the
Ghosts were scattered through several
enclaves across the city, that meant making

several flitter trips, each time evading any Seccie patrols. Ali had become skilled at piloting a flitter but by the time her shift was over she felt ready to collapse.

She went through the routine security checks on autopilot as she guided the flitter into the Fortress: the building Raven had purchased from the Countess to be their center of operations. Despite the strangeness of the arrangement she had never felt comfortable with moving away from the living space she shared with the other members of the original group. As she made her way up to the suite of rooms that she had designed Ali found herself wondering how long she would continue to call the Fortress home. Working for the group had been the focus of her life so much recently that she didn't often think about the future. Things had changed so much for her that the Fortress was the only real stability she knew and she was nervous of losing it.

Upstairs the sound of music filled the air, Avalon's voice mingling with a blend of multiple melodies that seemed to burn their way into her brain. As she entered the main living area the music died away and Avalon looked up, smiling. She was plainly dressed, her flame of red hair tied back in a long braid, but she still looked exotic, surrounded by a web of wiring connecting her and her guitar to a cluster of electronic devices.

"Hi," Ali said, flopping lifelessly into one of the chairs. "I hope I'm not disturbing you?"

"No." Avalon shook her head. "I'm just fooling about. Nothing serious yet."

"You're sounding good though," Ali replied, trying to persuade her tired mind to say something intelligent about the music. "It's haunting, as if I've remembered it before I've heard it . . ."

Avalon looked thoughtful and she picked out a few chords on her guitar before replying.

"Maybe you have," she said slowly. "Raven's idea was for me to try to portray the Hex abilities in music. Teaching the blind to see, she called it."

"That's it." Ali nodded. "It sounds like that's what you've done."

"Not just me." Avalon shook her head. "Raven wrote some of the lyrics."

"She did?" Ali's surprise was echoed by another voice overlapping with hers from the doorway and she turned to see Wraith, looking almost as tired as she felt. "I had no idea," he said, frowning a little. "Is this for the disk you're going to release to the underground?"

"That's right." Avalon fingered a few

more chords silently. "A sequel to 'Transformations.' Of course, the record company would sue me if they could, but being hunted by the government is no reason to stop making music."

"I didn't realize you were going to release it," Ali said, feeling herself waking up a little. "Whose idea was that?"

"Cloud's," Wraith explained. "He said Avalon may as well make the best of being a pariah and use her skills to the advantage of the group. The plan is to release it over the net and use Avalon's popularity to promote our cause."

"It's a good idea," Ali agreed. "But I'm surprised Raven's involved." She felt a flash of an old jealousy as she added: "I didn't realize she could write lyrics."

"I don't know if that's what I'd call them," Avalon said thoughtfully. "But you know how Raven talks, as if she's descending from another sphere where they communicate differently. I asked her what she thought about Hexes and wrote down what she said. It seemed to work."

"When are you releasing it?" Wraith asked and Avalon shrugged.

"Soon, I think," she said. "I've recorded all the tracks. Raven said she'd release it when the time seemed most auspicious, but that could mean anything."

"Where is Raven?" Wraith asked, glancing about the room as if he expected her to suddenly appear.

Ali and Avalon both shrugged. Aside from teaching sessions and mission briefings, Ali didn't see very much of Raven anyway. She didn't think anyone did.

Raven was at Dragon's Nest. The old Anglecynn base was in the depths of the city and because of its gloomy position in the heart of London's darkness, half-buried under the fragmentary detritus of the hundreds of levels above, it was the safest of the Ghost enclaves. Nowadays few people lived there. It was a base for what had once been Anglecynn's administrative staff: those people who preferred to fight for freedom from behind the lines. The rambling buildings had become the security center for the Ghosts. Every piece of data picked up from the surveillance tech, with which Raven had decorated every Ghost enclave in the city, ended up here; it was studied, discussed, reported on and filed.

It was also here, in the old meeting room, that Alaric had chosen to discuss his plan to sabotage the Security Services' communications network. He, Geraint, Jordan,

Raven, and Cloud sat on the ancient furniture, drinking coffee from a damaged Nutromac and discussing how to strike against the security arm of the Federation.

"The real problem as I see it," Alaric explained, "is that the Seccies don't get their orders from a single source."

"Surely they do?" Jordan looked confused."Seccies are responsible to the Minister for Internal Security, just as Fed Troopers are responsible to the Minister for Peace. Orders from Versailles in both cases."

"The Minister just formulates policy," Geraint objected. "Actual orders come from the civil service, they're just as culpable when considering Seccie crimes."

"I thought we were considering communications," Cloud pointed out and earned himself a narrow look from Geraint but Alaric continued as if none of the interruptions had occurred.

"Policy comes from Versailles and so do direct orders," he said. "But all actual communications travel a variety of routes through the net. It's not possible to stop messages getting through when they fly night and day, twenty-four hours. Seccies in England are connected to the rest of Europe. We make a move and their best minds are on to us."

"Surely the Hexes are an immense

advantage?" Jordan said, looking anxiously toward Raven who had not spoken yet and was watching the by-play with unreadable obsidian eyes.

"An advantage when there are enough of them, maybe," Alaric said slowly. "But at the moment, forgive me, Raven, there just aren't enough. We have to bypass increasingly sophisticated security to find out the CPS execution dates, which doesn't leave much time to keep watch on the Seccies and still less to strike back against them." He looked ruefully at Raven. "I know *you* can hack any system ever created," he said. "But there's only one of you."

"An indubitable fact," Raven agreed. "Cut to the chase, Alaric. What are you suggesting?"

"You know more about the data network than I do," Alaric said with a shrug. "But if there was some way to cut the communications line between Versailles and London the Seccies here would be blind and stumbling. No orders. No arrests."

Raven drummed her fingers on the side of her chair, thinking. The others looked at her hopefully. It was a look she was coming to recognize. These people came up with ideas but as usual they relied upon her to implement them. To them she was a sorceress, her capabilities a mystery, and the thought of her failing was impossible. It was a look Kez had given her when the CPS had captured them: behind the fear an absolute certainty that she would survive. Raven accepted it but she didn't encourage it. She relied on no one and it was independence she respected. But Alaric's idea was promising and her mind was already constructing a plan.

"The net is our problem as much as theirs," she mused aloud. "While their communications are always vulnerable to a Hex, the network is so vast a mesh that we can't control enough of it. Revenge burnt out when she tried to control just the section in this city and EF communications span the world."

Alaric nodded, thinking of the net stretched across the world like prison bars; controlling information, money and politics. "It's colossal," he said. "And they can send messages anywhere."

"Anywhere," Raven echoed. "But—"

"But?" Jordan was grinning admiringly, certain that Raven had an idea, and dark eyes turned to meet hers with an amused glint.

"But . . ." she continued, "there is a stop every message from the EF makes, no matter where it's coming from or going to."

The others looked blank but Cloud was

frowning thoughtfully. "The orbitals!" he exclaimed suddenly and turned to Raven for confirmation. She was smiling.

"Data doesn't travel along roads," she said. "It flies. Bounces off the earth and back thousands of times a second across the orbital satellite network."

"How many satellites are there?" Jordan asked, wide-eyed.

"About five hundred," Geraint replied automatically. "Different sizes and specifications, naturally."

"But all those satellites are controlled from one place," Raven reminded him.

"The EF Space Operations Center," Cloud added, and they all paused for thought.

"It's brilliant," Alaric said finally. "The EF aren't interested in space—the drive for the stars was abandoned over a hundred years ago as uneconomical. The American continent tried for a little longer but not much came of it. Some mining projects was all and then their program shut down as well."

"No one considers space," Geraint agreed. "I hadn't even thought of it myself. But you're right. Everything goes through the satellites and Space Ops controls them."

"There are problems though," Raven pointed out, bringing them all back to reality. "The Space Center is a shielded system. High security. And the computers that control the satellites aren't linked to the net. They function differently."

"We'd have to go there," Alaric said slowly and Raven nodded.

"To Transcendence," she said softly. "That's where it is."

"Transcendence?" Cloud raised an eyebrow. "That won't be easy."

Raven didn't answer him, her mind was already miles away. Transcendence: the European megaplex, the largest city in the world. A sprawling conglomerate of finance and politics where EF law ruled every inch of its gleaming spires and snaking corridors. In Transcendence artifice ruled; nothing was left to nature and everything came under the all-seeing eye of the electronic cyclops: constantly under surveillance by Seccies. But the thought of it drew her irresistibly. It was the triumph of the information age and, to her, the ultimate challenge.

It was almost dawn by the time Raven left Dragon's Nest. They had stayed up for hours discussing possible ways of getting to Transcendence but had finally adjourned, knowing that nothing could be decided before other senior members of the group had been consulted. As Raven and Cloud headed out of the room Jordan caught them up and touched Raven's arm lightly.

"Do you have a few more minutes?" she asked hopefully. "A security matter."

"A few minutes won't make much difference," Raven replied. "What is it?"

"We had a minor alert earlier today," Jordan explained, leading them toward the vast observational room. Vidscreens were mounted on every wall, currently showing nighttime views of the city. "A ganger kid wandered through one of the Ghost enclaves. Nothing major. But he could have been a scout for a serious incursion."

"Doubtful," Raven replied. "But show me anyway."

Jordan touched some keys on one of the terminals and a large vidscreen brightened, showing a display of a Ghost enclave on the edge of ganger territory.

"Kez called it in," Jordan explained. "There they are now."

Raven and Cloud watched silently as the small figures of Ali and Kez walked down an abandoned street. Neither of them looked at the surveillance cameras, absorbed in their own discussion. Then another figure appeared, dressed in black and silver, moving cautiously across the level.

"Give me a close-up," Raven said and

Jordan expanded the image to focus on the boy's face. Silver eyes turned to regard the watchers and Jordan whispered:

"He looked directly at several of the surveillance devices. Remember it was a policy that some should be made obvious for intimidation purposes?"

"Good-looking kid," Raven commented, the blend of human and machine appealing to her.

"There seems to be a computer terminal nesting in his hair," Cloud said dryly and Jordan grinned.

"I asked some of the people here if they could ID him," she said. "One of the Snakes said he looked like a Chrome. Have you heard of them?"

Raven shook her head. For the most part gangers didn't interest her. Their posturing and struggles for dominance bored her and she had no need for the sense of group identity they offered.

"I've heard of the Chromes," Cloud said, to their surprise. "They're a hacker gang somewhere in the middle levels."

"How would you know that?" Raven asked curiously and Cloud smiled.

"All megastars have their vices, don't they? Mine was holocam tech. I bought some items on the black market a few years back from the Chromes."

"Did they work?" Raven asked, a thoughtful look in her dark eyes.

"Like a dream," Cloud told them. "Had to leave it all behind though."

"Interesting." Raven turned back to the vidcam still. "What else does he do?"

"After he looked around for a while he got scared and ran off," Jordan told her, keying the image into motion so they could watch the boy's flight across the level. "What do you think?"

"I think you were right to disregard it as a threat," Raven replied. "But it's interesting nonetheless. I think I may have occasion to find out more about this gang."

Looking consideringly at the vidcam she regarded the Chrome boy with an almost avaricious expression. She smiled to herself as she added:

"It's been a long time since I met a hacker who wasn't a Hex."

3

Fled into the Wilderness

Tally awoke a little before dawn. Last night they had given her mother's dead body to the sea. Now she sat on the roof and watched the remorseless waves lapping against the palazzo as if trying to claim her and Gift as well. The rising sun stained the sky a bloody red, bruised streaks of light emanating from one glowing point in a velvety dark night. Turning her back on it, she looked northwest, toward England. It seemed like an impossible journey through the heart of the Federation's power. Gift was confident they would make it but Tally had doubts. Sometimes when she closed her eyes she could feel the data net in the air. Strands of information stretching like tentacles to encompass the world. But she couldn't touch it or control it, and without that ability it would find her and destroy her.

She shivered at the thought of it, huddling deeper into her blanket and heard Gift speak behind her.

"You shouldn't come out here so early if you're cold."

"I'm not cold. I'm worried," she corrected him. "I'm concerned about this journey we've got to make. This journey which we have no idea how to start."

"Don't be so negative," Gift reprimanded her. "Look what I've found." She turned to look and saw him extending a small silver case toward her. "I found it last night," he said, lowering his voice to a whisper despite the deserted city.

Tally touched an almost hidden catch on the side of the case and it slid open to reveal a single computer disk, held in place by two clips. It didn't look particularly special but Gift was gazing at it with a kind of reverence.

"It's useless if we can't access it," she pointed out and her twin frowned, snatching the case back.

"It's our legacy," he objected. "Weren't you listening last night? With this we can rule the world."

"I don't want to rule the world!" Tally objected fiercely. "I want to be a normal kid who goes to school and has parents and doesn't have to run halfway across Europe because people want to kill me for a power I don't even know how to use!"

Realizing that her voice was rising to a shriek, she clapped a hand over her mouth and stopped speaking. For a few moments Gift said nothing. Then he put an arm around her gently.

"It's OK," he said soothingly. "We'll find a way. Come on, Tally. You're as smart as I am and I need you to help me. This is something we have to do. Help me think of how to do it."

Tally resisted the urge to snap that she'd thought he had it all planned out. She knew that he had lied to their mother as much as she had, pretending a confidence neither of them felt so that Harmony could die in peace. But now she had never felt so alone and she stayed silent for a while as she gathered the energy to begin again.

The sun rose slowly while Tally thought. They had been hiding for most of their lives: in abandoned cities or in the few wildernesses left in the technological age. Ignorant of the secret history behind their flight, they had known only that they were hunted. Through those long years Gift had fueled his rage against the Federation and vowed many times to strike back in revenge for the death of their father, murdered by Seccies while Harmony had escaped with the twins. But Tally only felt weary and she wondered where she would find the strength to obey her mother's last wishes. The Hexes in England seemed immeasurably distant and she didn't even know if they had the knowledge to help them. But with that thought suddenly her muddle of ideas resolved themselves.

"If these other Hexes can help us when we get to England perhaps they can aid us before then," she said slowly. Gift looked confused.

"How?" he asked. "They don't even know we exist yet."

"Yes, but we could tell them," Tally replied. "If we can access a computer terminal we could send them a message. Tell them who we are and that we need their help."

"But we don't know who they are," Gift said, shaking his head. "It's a good idea but I can't see how it would work, Tally."

"Mother said a Hex could set their mind free in the net. That we have the ability to send our consciousness into the data network. If we were to do that—"

"We might find one of them!" Gift said, completing her thought. "Tally, that's brilliant!"

"It won't be easy." Tally mused. "We'll have to get access to a terminal first and figure out how to use it. But it'll be a lot easier than trying to cross Europe on our own and it might just work."

"We should go to Padua," Gift said decisively. "It's the nearest city and we'll be able to find a terminal there."

"But we'll have to be careful," Tally said firmly. "If anyone were to find out about the disk we'd be in greater danger than ever before."

It was late in the morning when Ali woke up to the sound of her vidcom chiming and the realization that she had overslept. Stumbling out of bed, she found the key to activate the unit and blinked sleepily as Luciel's face appeared on the screen.

"Late night?" he asked sympathetically.

"Yeah," Ali said, rubbing the sleep from her eyes. "Is it me or are Seccie patrols getting more common?"

Luciel laughed as he replied. "You're not spending enough time with Alaric, obviously," he said. "He's been talking about nothing else for weeks. According to Jordan he had a meeting with Raven last night about what to do about it."

"I heard he had some kind of plan," Ali

admitted. "But I didn't know it had anything to do with Raven."

"Everything has something to do with Raven," Luciel pointed out. "Like today's mission for instance. The one you're running late for?"

"Mission," Ali frowned, trying to remember what was on her schedule for today.

"The extraction?" Luciel prompted. "Another game of beat the Seccies to the Hex?"

"Right," Ali said, remembering. "Sorry. How late am I?"

"Seeing as the Raven has yet to put in an appearance you can have a whole ten minutes to suit up," Luciel said with a grin. "Seeya soon."

The vidcam image dissolved into black and Ali hunted through her closet for her combat fatigues. Once she would have taken hours getting dressed in the morning, designing her outfits to conform exactly to the current dictates of fashion. Now she struggled into the loose fatigues without a second thought, scraping her hair back with a hasty plait, and holstering the regulation issue blaster. Catching a glimpse of herself in the mirror as she headed out the door she grinned, imagining what her old clique of popular pretty friends would say if they could see her now.

She ran down the stairs and emerged in the main room of the building just in time to add herself to the end of the line for equipment checks. Luciel was conducting the check-through and, as Ali waited for her turn, she glanced down the line to see who else was part of the extraction team. There were more and more Ghosts she didn't recognize. But Daniel grinned at her from halfway down the line and Ali smiled back. Daniel had joined the group through Anglecynn, voluntarily throwing away a life of luxury for his principles and giving enough government secrets to the terrorists to ensure that he could never go back. Ali liked him partly because their backgrounds were so similar. No matter how close she had become to the other Ghosts she still sometimes felt adrift in the urban wastelands many of them had come from.

Her attention was called back when Luciel came to a halt in front of her and she quickly offered her weapon for inspection. The equipment checks were for their own safety and had quickly become part of the established routine after the Hexes had joined up with Anglecynn. The terrorist faction had changed the character of the group by bringing a military precision to arrangements that made this extraction seem like routine.

Also routine was the fact that Raven was late. She appeared in the flitter bay just as Luciel pronounced the check complete, dressed in black as usual with equipment of different shapes and sizes tucked into the voluminous pockets of her loose overcoat. Luciel didn't ask to check her equipment and Ali didn't expect him to. Raven was a law unto herself where regulations were concerned and no one was willing to push the point. Not even acknowledge their presence, her dark eyes unreadable as usual, Raven slung herself into the pilot's seat and turned to glare at the other members of the team.

"Well?" she demanded. "What are you waiting for?"

"Nothing," Luciel replied quickly, answering for all of them and hurrying the group forward into the flitter. "Let's get moving, people." He turned to Raven to add: "The CPS haven't picked up on this one yet so it should be easy in and out."

Raven only grunted in reply and, making haste to get into the flitter, Ali realized with a jab of discomfort that as the last to board she had been left with the unenviable position of sitting next to Raven. Swallowing her misgivings she strapped herself into the seat, knowing Raven's reputation as a pilot too well for comfort. The black-haired Hex was already powering up the streamlined flying craft as its doors hissed shut and, without any signal from the team, the main doors of the Fortress opened in perfect synchronicity.

Ali glanced quickly at the younger Hex. One thin pale hand was resting on the control panel of the flitter, the other was drumming impatiently on the armrest as the bay doors opened slowly to their full extent. Raven used her abilities casually and, despite her obvious bad mood, the team relaxed slightly. An extraction mission, no matter how routine, was often tricky but Raven's presence lent them confidence. To many of the Ghosts, especially the newcomers, she was already a legend. Ali had heard Kez telling some of the younger children stories that made it sound as if Raven had single-handedly saved every Hex in the group and beaten half the Federation army while doing it.

"It's harmless," Luciel had said when she objected. "Regardless of her flaws, Raven has achieved more than any of us. Seeing her as a legend encourages people and we should use every advantage we have."

Ali hadn't pursued the subject any further, not wanting to appear jealous. But, looking at Rave now, she wondered if she had been wrong not to continue the argument. Raven looked immeasurably distant, her mind linked to the net, and for the first time Ali wondered if Raven had become so much of a legend that she was no longer real to any of them.

A sudden jolt threw her back into her seat as the flitter took off; Raven judging the moment perfectly so that the aerial crafts swooped through the bay doors with only an inch of clearance and shot out into the ganglands. Ali heard a couple of muffled exclamations in the back of the flitter, probably from team members who had never experienced the way Raven drove before. Used to the dizzying speed, she tried to relax and concentrate on the mission ahead as Luciel ran through the mission brief one last time.

"We'll be going to a closed community in the heights called Fairseat," Luciel explained. "There won't be much Seccie surveillance because it has its own security for all the VIPs who live there but we will have to evade them once we're inside."

"How are we getting inside?" a team member Ali didn't recognize asked and Luciel replied:

"The plan is to go through the service entrance."

Ali frowned at that. She'd lived in a similar complex until a few years ago and it wasn't as if the place had been swarming with service personnel. Even if it had been, she reflected, they wouldn't have looked much like the team she was with now. It was too late to raise objections but if she'd been in charge of the mission she would have made more of an effort to construct a team that could blend into the background in the milieu of the ultra-rich.

"Our target is a twelve-year-old Hex named Charis Weaver," Luciel was continuing. "And if her family's movements are consistent, she'll be in today and her parent's won't be. Should be easy, like I said."

"Well stop saying it," Raven cut in suddenly. "I'm not working with a team that thinks an extraction is a breeze, you scan?"

"Sure, Raven," Luciel said in a mollifying tone. "I understand."

"You had better," Raven added and glanced across at Ali as if to enforce her command. But Ali had no disagreement with the order and met the black eyes seriously. They regarded her searchingly for a moment and then, to Ali's surprise, returned to the view ahead without Raven saying anything.

The rest of the team had fallen silent and they remained so as Raven guided the flitter up through the levels of the city and settled down to a slow cruising speed as they reached the heights. As they approached a five-level high complex faced in gleaming white stone and surrounded by gated walls, Ali had a sense of foreboding. Most of the extractions she had been on had been from poorer areas of the city. This castlelike edifice was an entirely different proposition. Fairseat was truly a closed community, without the usual conduits and grav-tubes for people and vehicles to enter from the levels above and below. Instead, the complex rested on a huge flat expanse of gleaming plazas and gardens and was closed off at the top of its levels by a similar shining ceiling. No natural light would penetrate into this community but Ali somehow doubted that the inhabitants considered that a priority. They lived in the heights for the prestige of the location, not to be closer to the sun.

Raven cruised around the side of the complex and then moved away again, circling up and around to the next level. Ali could hear random clinks and jingles as the team adjusted their weapons and equipment. Then, as lightly as a feather, the flitter touched down at the side of a graceful archway and Raven cut the power.

"We're here," she said quietly. "The service exit is just behind this arch."

The doors slid open with a soft sigh from the hydraulics. The level they were on was almost deserted and the team climbed out quietly, wary of disturbing the peace. Luciel ushered them around the side of the bridge as Raven keyed the flitter's security system on and, following the rest of the team, Ali came to a halt in front of a large metal door. It had no obvious lock and she wondered how they were expected to get in but Raven, appearing behind her, gave a low laugh.

"Computer-controlled," she said with a wry smile. "Lucky for us they don't learn." She looked at Ali for a moment and then at Luciel. "One of you want to give it a go?"

"I don't think so," Ali said quickly and Raven raised an eyebrow ironically.

"Luciel?" she asked and the boy stepped forward, placing the palm of his hand against the door.

"Good," Raven acknowledged. "Now feel the circuitry. It runs through the entire door and leads back to a controlling security system. Follow the flow of current back to the system and order the door to open."

Luciel closed his eyes and the rest of the team watched silently as they waited for him. He was biting his lips, his expression anxious as he attempted to feel his way to the net: a skill that Raven had attempted to teach all of them but without much success. Finally he broke away from the door and opened his eyes.

"It's no good," he said, shaking his head. "I can't reach it."

"Very well," said Raven expressionlessly. "Move out of the way."

Reaching toward the door she rested her fingertips on it lightly. The rest of the team held their breath and almost instantaneously there was an audible click and the door swung open.

"Why didn't she do that in the first place?" someone muttered behind Ali and was rapidly hushed.

"Come on," Luciel said, to cover the moment of awkwardness. "Let's go." Then, leading the way, he entered the long curving tunnel ahead of them. Ali trailed behind the rest of the team; last except for Raven who closed the door behind her. The dark-haired girl regarded her in the dim light.

"You should have tried," she said.

"If I spent my life learning how, I could still never do what you do," Ali replied, keeping her voice low. "You know that."

For a few moments there was silence, broken only by the sound of the team trooping down the corridor. Then Raven spoke, her voice almost a whisper.

"If the responsibility for failure isn't yours, it's your teacher's," she said softly. "And I don't want it."

Then, like a shadow, she moved ahead in the line; disappearing down into the darkness ahead where Ali could no longer see her.

There was an elevator at the end of the corridor and Luciel was able to summon it by fiddling with the keypad that controlled it.

"This leads down to the ventilation system," he explained.

"And the kid's sure to be wandering around the ventilation system," Ali muttered under her breath and received a sharp look from Raven.

"You see a flaw with the plan?" she asked softly, as they crowded into the elevator.

"I hope not," Ali replied quietly, reluctant to say anything but convinced that if there was a problem Raven should know about it. Leaning closer to Raven so the others wouldn't hear she continued, "This kind of complex doesn't like to have a lot of staff wandering about. They like to be served invisibly and from a distance. And security looks really tight here."

She looked at Raven, half hoping the other girl would tell her she was wrong but she had narrowed her eyes thoughtfully.

"You may well be right," she murmured. "But stay chill." Then she moved away and rested a hand on the side of the elevator car, her eyes glazing over as she sank into communion with whatever computer system was controlling it. Ali watched her anxiously, hoping that Raven would know what to do if they did run into trouble. Luciel was a good team leader but he didn't have Raven's experience or her inventiveness and, despite her uncomfortable relationship with the younger Hex, Raven had saved both their lives with her skill before.

The elevator touched down and the doors slid open, revealing an empty room. The team fanned out around it and Luciel moved to the door and opened it cautiously, one hand on his stun gun.

"It's clear," he said and the others moved to join him.

The room beyond was obviously a control room—banks of terminals were set into the walls of intervals and screens showed complicated read-outs which Ali assumed pertained to the ventilation system. A single grav-tube led down into the complex itself. The room was dominated by one large window and she moved to it instinctively.

Taking a look outside, her throat clenched with alarm and she looked back at the others, still inspecting the terminals.

"Raven?" she said. "Come and look at this."

The other girl moved to join her at the window and together they looked down on the Fairseat community. It was like a miniature city, bringing back memories for Ali of the Belgravia complex in which she had grown up. White buildings flowed into each other in a stylish architectural design, linked by balconies and walkways softened with a cascade of greenery. Slender trees grew up from the floor, five levels below, and almost reached the ceiling.

"Remind you of home, Ali?" Daniel said suddenly from behind them. "Looks so restful, doesn't it?"

"Yes, it does," Ali admitted. But the anxiety hadn't left her and she was watching Raven for a response.

"Luciel," Raven said, summoning the boy over from the other side of the room. "Tell me again where our target lives."

"Westview Tower," he replied, coming over to join them at the window. "Second level." He looked out across the complex, orienting himself. "Just over there," he added, waving an arm to indicate one of the white skyscraper sections. "We'll cross that archway and then go in through that portico."

"You have to be kidding," Ali blurted out. "We'll be seen!"

"There's plenty of cover," Luciel replied, pointing out the trees beneath them. "And we'll be moving fast."

"We'll be dead meat," Raven said and Ali sighed in relief that the other Hex agreed with her.

"What do you mean?" Luciel protested and Raven turned to face him.

"Even if we're not seen by a single human being, this kind of complex has surveillance specifically intended to prevent strangers from breaking in. The second a vidcam sees us we'll be locked in and it will take all the firepower we have to blast our way out again."

"Should we go back then?" Daniel asked.

Raven thought for a moment and the others watched her expectantly. Even Luciel knew that if Raven didn't want to continue there would be no point in carrying on without her. Finally the Hex shook her head.

"No, we can go on," she said. "But carefully. And only a few of us."

"What about the surveillance?" Ali asked and Raven smiled slightly.

"I think I have an idea to prevent it from seeing us," she said. "If it works out it may prove useful in another mission Alaric is planning. Ali, you and Daniel come with me. Luciel, can you and the others stay here and you start hacking into the system. If there is an alert we'll need you to keep this way out open for us."

"Understood," Luciel replied. "Good luck then."

Raven nodded and then turned to Ali and Daniel.

"Come on," she said and led them toward the grav-tube.

As they descended into the Fairseat complex Raven closed out all external distractions and concentrated on her link to the net. Without touching the security system she could feel it surrounding her like a cage. Invisible eyes watched the complex from all directions and the path they would need to take across it would bring them into full view of the hidden vidcams. Although she could easily block those signals, preventing the cameras from seeing anything but static, that would trigger an alert as much as the sight of their intrusion. So instead she reached for those cameras and concentrated on what they should be seeing. The visual images they transmitted were encoded as data and delicately Raven reached for that datastream. It flowed smoothly and irresistibly toward the security control room for the complex, buried deep in the maze of graceful buildings. With infinite care Raven reached out with her mind toward the net and diverted the path of the stream, bringing it around in a loop and then feeding the loop back to the control room. By the time the grav-tube had touched the floor of the complex the vidcams were under her control, showing only empty space where they walked: their true transmissions blocked by the loop she had created.

"We'll have to move fast," she said, and her companions nodded their assent.

They crossed the complex like ghosts, unseen by the vidcams and ducking smoothly out of sight when another human approached. Staying under the cover of the trees they moved toward Westview Tower. As they entered the ornamental portico that concealed the entrance, the doors ahead slid open at Raven's unspoken command and they hurried into the cool confines of the complex. The corridor ahead of them was lavishly decorated with carefully placed ornaments chosen for their expense as much as their beauty. Here they couldn't hide from people and all three of them concealed their weapons, trying to walk as if they belonged there. Raven continued to fool the vidcams but she knew that if one of the passersby raised an alert her work would have been futile. However, although they received a few puzzled looks, no one stopped them and challenged their right to be there. Raven led them unerringly toward the apartment where Charis Weaver lived and within ten minutes they stood outside the door.

"Security system registers one person inside," Raven said. "Young female, twelve years of age, looks like our target."

"Let's go and get her then," Daniel said with relief, and Raven keyed the apartment doors open.

They stepped inside to find themselves in a suite of rooms no less lavish than the rest of the complex. A vidscreen in front of them showing a popular drama Ali vaguely remembered: a vid program about a group of kids who helped Seccies catch criminals. It was not a promising omen and the girl who stood looking at them in the center of the room was even less promising. She was dressed with a casual style that was too perfect to be anything other than expensive and her honey-blonde curls were caught up in an artistically tumbled heap. Her blue eyes were wide as she looked at them but her voice was cool and controlled as she asked:

"What are you doing in my apartment?"

"We've come to rescue you," Daniel began. "We know you're a Hex and we—"

"Well, I don't want to be rescued," the girl told them firmly. "Go away or I'll call security."

"Don't do that!" Daniel exclaimed. "Please, hear me out?"

"Okay," she said slowly. "But don't come near me." To lend emphasis to her words she crossed to the terminal, where she could summon security if she wanted to.

"Raven?" Ali asked quietly, wondering if the other Hex's control over the system was strong enough to prevent the girl from getting a message out.

"Possibly," Raven replied, under her breath, understanding what Ali wanted to know. "But don't expect miracles."

Daniel was trying to stay calm and he extended his hands as unthreateningly as he could toward the kid, showing her that they were empty.

"It's okay," he told her. "We're not here to hurt you, really." He hesitated. "You are Charis Weaver, aren't you?"

"Yes, that's me," the girl replied warily.

"Okay, Charis," Daniel continued. "Look, we want to help you. If the CPS find out you're a Hex, your life will be in danger. But if you come with us you'll be safe."

"I don't want to come with you," Charis told him definitely. "My parents will look after me. I don't need you."

"Charis—" Daniel began, but she was shaking her head vigorously.

"No!" she said, her voice rising slightly. "I don't want to. Just go away!"

Daniel swung around and looked at the others with an expression of helplessness.

"Raven," he said. "You tell her."

"Dammit, Daniel, leave me out of it!" Raven snapped, her eyes flashing black fire. "Just for once don't expect me to solve all the problems. If the kid wants to stay, let her stay. Maybe she'll be safer here. What am I supposed to know about it?"

"Raven!" Daniel's voice was exasperated but Ali stopped him from continuing.

"Be quiet," she told him, her voice unexpectedly firm. "Raven's right. This isn't her problem. It's mine."

4

The Voice of Many Waters

Tally and Gift had traveled the route between Venice and Padua before: concealed in the back of an ancient skimmer whose owner had been paid almost all their mother had to transport them with no questions asked. Now they would have to travel alone and from the edge of the massive road Tally watched the traffic pass and wondered how they would manage it. The skimmer expressway wound its way through the sleepy Italian countryside like a roaring monster. Thirty lanes of traffic coiled around each other in a helix of sound and speed overlooked by the flitter lanes above where tiny silver specks made a ribbon of light in the sky.

All the possessions the children owned

were tied up in a dirty backpack and Gift carried the precious data disk next to his heart. No one could see them from the expressway but, even if they had, two scruffy children would attract no attention. That would be different in the city where beggars and transients would be stopped and questioned by the local Seccies. Turning away from the monstrous flood of skimmers, Tally looked at Gift.

"This is useless," she said. "We'd better turn away from the expressway and head for one of the smaller country roads. We might find someone willing to give us a lift."

"Mother always said that wasn't safe," Gift objected.

"Well she's not here to say that now, is she?" Tally snapped. "And how are we expected to cross Europe walking? Last I heard, England is still an island."

"OK, OK," Gift said placatingly. "But let's be careful. Do you have your knife somewhere you can reach it?"

Tally checked the thin blade tucked into a sheath at the side of her boot and adjusted it slightly.

"I have it," she said. "But I hope I don't have to use it."

"On Seccies?" Gift said with a grim smile. "I'll look forward to it."

"And that will make us *so* much better than them," Tally said sarcastically. "Don't joke about killing people, Gift. It isn't funny."

"Maybe I'm not joking," Gift replied, his voice low and dangerous.

Tally sighed, not wanting to get into another argument about it.

"Come on," she said. "Let's go and find another road."

Gift hoisted the backpack and they set off but, as they walked, Tally worried about her brother. She was sure that his hate for the Federation would get him into trouble and she didn't know if she'd be able to help him when it came.

Ignoring Raven and Daniel, Ali concentrated on the child in front of her. She knew how Charis felt with an empathy that surprised her. None of their other extractions had been this difficult. Most of the time they arrived seconds ahead of the CPOS and the children were grateful to be rescued. Sometimes their parents had thanked the Ghosts for taking them, other times they had cursed their children for being mutants. In both cases the parting was difficult but Ali had never encountered a Hex who didn't want to be rescued before. However, looking around the apartment that reminded her so much of her old home, Ali could understand why.

Concentrating her attention on Charis, she tried to focus her thoughts.

"I understand why you don't want to leave," she said. "I used to be just like you. Nothing ever goes wrong here, does it? Within these walls you're perfectly safe."

"Yes, I am," Charis insisted. "I don't even know how you got in here."

"We were able to get in because we are Hexes," Ali said quietly. "And there's no computer system in the world that's safe from us, even the security system of Fairseat."

"Then I'm *not* like you," Charis said, with an expression of relief. "I can't do things like that. I'm just good with computers, that's all. I'm not really a Hex."

"No, you can't do things like that," Ali agreed. "But you are a Hex. In the eyes of the European Federation, the CPS and the Seccies, you *are* a Hex and you should know what that means as well as we do."

"You think I'll be caught," Charis replied. "but what if I'm not? She said I might be OK." She glanced at Raven nervously.

"Yes, you might be fine," Ali told her. "You might be able to live the rest of your life being perfectly safe within these walls. But then again you might not."

She took a long breath, remembering how she had felt when Raven revealed that she knew her secret. She'd thought she was trapped but it wasn't until she'd joined the other Hexes that she had realized she'd never been free before.

"Charis, I was once just like you and I thought I could keep my secret forever. I didn't want to leave home either. But one day the CPS came for me. They took me away while my father watched and there was nothing he could do."

She didn't go into detail about the experimental lab they had taken her to. There were some things that could be explained to Charis later if she chose to come with them and there were others that were too horrible to speak of.

"Raven rescued me, Charis," Ali explained, turning to look back briefly at the other girl. "She saved me from the CPS, she saved a friend of mine and she's saved hundreds of other kids since then. Raven's the best there is. Even the government knows it and some day she'll force them to give us our rights as real people. But in the meantime you're *not* safe. You won't ever be safe so long as you're a Hex and trying to keep it a secret. Wouldn't you rather come with us now than wake up some morning with the CPS at the gates of Fairseat and know that we can't save you in time?" She looked at Charis straight in the eyes as she finished. "We can't force you to come with us and we won't try but they can and they will and there will be nothing you or your parents can do about it."

Ali stopped speaking, realizing that she'd said everything she could, and just waited. Charis looked back at her, her face pale and serious as her eyes moved from Ali to Daniel to Raven. Finally she spoke.

"Can I leave a letter for my parents?"

"Yes, if you want to," Ali replied as Daniel heaved a sigh of relief. "But please be quick, we don't have much time."

"I'll go and pack," Charis said and headed for one of the doors leading out of the room.

Once she had left Ali sat down on the side of one of the chairs, feeling immeasurably tired.

"Well done!" Daniel exclaimed. "I've never heard you talk like that before."

"Thank you," Ali said with a smile but it was Raven she turned to look at.

"Congratulations," Raven said softly and Ali felt a smile spread across her face as she looked at the younger Hex.

"You mean that?" she asked.

"Of course." The old snap was back in Raven's voice as she added: "I always say what I mean. Now go and hurry that kid up before this security system realizes what games I've been playing with it."

Alaric was already making plans to strike at the heart of the Federation's power. Raven's mention of the satellite network and the Space Operations Center in Transcendence had enthused him with a new passion for the cause and it was a natural move to seek out the only other member of the Ghosts with a similar fixation. He found Wraith in one of the smaller Ghost enclaves on the edge of the city with a group of the older Hex children. The slender ganger with his wild unnaturally white hair was an icon for the kids who were old enough to strike back against Seccie persecution. He taught them how to use weaponry and they imitated him almost slavishly dying their hair white to conform to their own image of what the Ghosts should be.

Watching Wraith surrounded by children with serious faces, holding their weapons of destruction with a practiced ease, Alaric was struck by how many of these kids there were now. They *are* the Ghosts, he thought to himself. Much more

than the members of Anglecynn of the
original Hex group ever were. These children outnumber us now and if we don't
succeed in finding them a future they'll do
it themselves. The thought was a little
daunting and it made him pause as he
watched the kids taking turns at blasting at
targets. Eventually the gunfire came to a
halt and Wraith ordered them to stand
down their weapons. As the kids obeyed
his instructions he came over to meet
Alaric.

"Didn't expect to see you here," he said
with a smile. "I thought you were busy plot-
ting to take over the world for us."

"Something like that," Alaric grinned
wryly, then glanced over at the children. "I
have a feeling these kids might get there
first though. You've taught them well."

"Too well, perhaps," Wraith replied seriously. "You lose something in your innocence when you're trained to kill, even if
you never use that knowledge."

"But if the choice is between innocence
or survival . . ." Alaric replied and Wraith
shrugged acceptingly.

"Agreed," he said. "We have no choice."

"Maybe not, but we do have options,"
Alaric replied. "And that's part of what I
want to talk to you about. I think I may
have an idea . . ."

● ● ●

Drow hadn't used the net since he'd first noticed the darkness, and he was curiously reluctant to touch the computer terminal. The black cloud that had ensnared him had haunted his dreams and he was constantly assailed by visions of drowning in pitch. But his father expected him to help test out the capabilities of the programs he had stolen and so he had resolved to face his fears.

Slotting another of the stolen disks in, he keyed on the terminal in his room and dived into the net. He was supposed to be fortifying his family's own computer system with the new encryption algorithms, setting up an unhackable password protocol, but after about an hour of work his mind began to drift, drawn by the strange affinity he felt for the network. Almost unconsciously he let his mind slip further and further away from the terminal he was working at, out through the computer system and on to one of the major highways of the net. Data traffic sped past him and he watched it flow by, simply enjoying the color and life around him. Sliding into a datastream he allowed himself to be carried along, soothed by the constant flow of information. Then, suddenly something off-kilter jarred him back into full awareness.

Nearby, an information node slowed and stopped winking as if it had been suddenly obscured. He turned to regard it, holding it in his mind, and saw it return. But in data milliseconds away a tendril of nothingness was curling past the datastreams, enfolding them in darkness and then sliding on.

Drow shivered, not wanting to follow that black tendril back to where it came from. The contagion was plainly spreading through the net and he didn't even know what it was, let alone what to do about it. He wondered about speaking to one of the other Chromes but he knew that none of them would interface with computers the way he did. The few times he had attempted to explain what he felt to one of them she had looked blank, unable to understand what he was describing. But maybe there was someone out there who could understand, somewhere in the vast reaches of the net. Withdrawing from the terminal, he considered the possibility. What he needed was to send the message to anyone who saw the net the way he did, a message only another person with his abilities could read. Slowly an idea began to occur to him and he sank back into the net as he considered it.

In all the net he was the only conscious entity that he knew of, unique among the mindless data signals. Using the skills he had learned while programming for the Chromes, he constructed a search program that would look for other anomalies, creatures in the flow of data that didn't behave the way data should. When his search program found one it would give them his message and where to look for him; a pre-arranged location in the net which he would check every day for a response. His search program complete, he keyed in his message.

>to those who the net sets free—something here is different—what is it that spreads darkness like a virus?—bring me your answer—if you exist <

Cloud knew something had changed when the team returned. He had been watching for them in the Ghost enclave, wanting to talk to Raven about her plan to go to Transcendence, but when the team returned he realized it might be the wrong time to speak to her. The others climbed eagerly out of the flitter, escorting a self-composed child carrying an expensive-looking sling bag. Daniel and Ali were chattering enthusiastically to her about Ghosts and Cloud watched the group pass him, completely absorbed in their own affairs. Once they had gone by he walked up to the small vehicle. Raven was sitting in the pilot's seat, staring into space and, after hesitating for a fraction of a second, Cloud swung himself into the seat beside her.

"Successful mission?" he asked and black eyes tracked slowly across to regard him.

"We rescued a child from dreams of luxury and offered her despair," Raven said bleakly.

"Sounds fairly standard," Cloud replied, trying to bring a measure of humor to the conversation. When Raven didn't reply he stayed silent, thinking.

"Why do you despair, Raven?" he said eventually. "What do you care for children's dreams?"

"I don't despair," Raven corrected him, an edge in her voice. "But I don't dream either."

"So our magician is a realist after all?"

"If only I can discover what is real," Raven replied.

"Sometimes I'm not certain you're real," Cloud told her. "So many of the others persist in thinking of you as a legend that I wonder if we invented you."

"I invented myself in the net and outside it I have to remember to exist."

"In that case you had better go and find

some reality," Cloud suggested. "Aren't you planning to unleash Avalon's new release on the world? Now's a good a time as any."

"Yes, I'll do that," Raven said definitely, moving gracefully out of the flitter. "It may well be time her words were heard."

"Her words or yours?" Cloud asked but Raven was already leaving and if she heard him she didn't answer.

Avalon was idly retuning her guitar and watching the holovid with the sound turned off when Ali and Luciel arrived in the Fortress, cheerful about having rescued another Hex.

"She's so self-possessed," Ali told her. "I'm sure she's going to be a really strong Hex."

"You just say that because that's what Raven's like," Luciel pointed out. "And the word isn't self-possessed, it's 'cold.' Even Wraith says he hardly knows her."

Avalon turned to look at them and Luciel caught her eye.

"Don't look disapproving," the singer told him. "I was just thinking about what you said. But if Raven's difficult to know it must be because she wants to be because she wants it that way."

"Why would anyone want to be that isolated?" Luciel objected. "Just because she likes it when people are afraid of her?"

"I'm not afraid of Raven," Ali objected. "Well, not much anyway."

"I don't believe Raven wants people to fear her," Avalon said and Ali nodded her agreement.

"Well in that case, what does she want?" Luciel asked.

"I think it's more a case of what she doesn't want," Avalon replied. "She doesn't want to be connected to other people. She resists it even with Wraith and he's the only family she has left."

"And that's why," Ali added, with a sudden flash of understanding. "Because he *is* the only family she has left. If she was connected to people she might lose them." She thought of her own father whom she hadn't seen since the day the CPS took her away.

"I don't think it's that simple," Avalon replied, shaking her head. "Although maybe that's part of it."

"What *do* you think then?" Luciel asked and Avalon shrugged.

"Raven was very young when she had to fend for herself," she said slowly. "I don't think she was able to form the normal connections to other people that most of us feel.

I think she connected to the net instead and that's why her Hex abilities are so strong. The net is her natural environment and the rest of her life is just marking time."

The others were silent as they considered the concept and Avalon continued to play with her guitar. After a few minutes Luciel opened his mouth to speak but was silenced when the holovid news feed suddenly displayed an image of Avalon.

"Where's the moment control?" he asked quickly, forgetting what he had been about to say. "You're on the vid, Avalon!"

Ali spotted the control first and keyed it on so that the news anchor's voice was projected into the room in midsentence:

". . . the singer Avalon, now a renegade on the run from the CPS since she joined a known terrorist group last year. Less than an hour ago a collection of music was released into the web on a variety of public bulletin boards and data feeds. The collection is entitled 'Deliberate Disguises,' a possible reference to the work of a twentieth-century poet, and the music is consistent with Avalon's style. Although the collection is almost certain to be proscribed by the government seeing as it is allegedly the work of a criminal, this station was able to access it before any ban comes into effect and our expert analysts are convinced that both the music and the voice of the singer belong to Avalon. However, the lyrics *of the songs are wildly dissimilar to any work produced by Masque, the band to which Avalon previously belonged."*

Ali and Luciel were glued to their seats as the commentary unfolded, fascinated by the news item as much because nothing like this had ever happened before as because it was something they were involved in. Having grown up in the world of media, Ali knew that the release of an underground music album was a rare event. The release of an underground album by a rock star-turned terrorist who had disappeared from view at the peak of her fame was a sensational event. Cloud had been right to suggest that Avalon's music was the greatest gift she could ever give to the Hex cause. The news feeds wouldn't be able to resist a story like this and every time it was mentioned it lent prominence and even respectability to the Hexes.

"We go now for comments from the other members of Masque: Lissa, Corin and Jesse," the announcer was saying and the vidscreen shifted into an image of the three musicians.

"I'm just relieved to know Avalon's alive," Corin said seriously, looking directly into the camera. *"We've all worried, not knowing what became of her or of Cloud. Now we know that, wherever they are, they're safe and still*

creating music. Avalon's still the most talented musician in the business and nothing's going to change that."

"*She's also fighting for something she believes in—*" Jesse added but was cut off abruptly by the interviewer who asked:

"*What about you, Lissa? What do you think of the album?*"

"*I wish Avalon was with us,*" Lissa replied, with a sorrowful expression. "*She's an electric musician but without the rest of the group she's missing something. Masque complemented Avalon. Together we created something beyond what any of us could have done individually. I'm sorry that she's given that up.*"

"*It's been suggested that she's collaborating with someone new,*" the interviewer pointed out. "*Do you believe that Avalon wrote those lyrics?*"

"*Most definitely not,*" Lissa said firmly. "*Those words are pure sedition. Avalon would never have described Hexes as 'prophets of possibility.' She wasn't even political.*"

"*Her views may have changed since she discovered she was a Hex—*" Jesse began to say, but then the image shifted again and returned to the face of the news anchor.

"*The disturbing content of the album means that we are unable to play it to you here but Avalon's album seems certain to rock the music world on its foundations. In this collection of songs she has achieved sounds beyond what has ever been created before. Our analysts are still unable to state what instruments are being played . . ."*

The sound on the vidscreen died as Avalon touched the moment control and Luciel and Ali turned to look at her.

"That's great!" Ali said, smiling. "It's really had an effect."

"I hope it's enough," Luciel added cautiously. "The news feed seemed very reluctant to actually discuss Hexes."

"People will be discussing it though," Ali pointed out. "Discussing it and speculating about what it really means to be a mutant. People loved Avalon. A lot of them won't stop just because she's a Hex."

"You think so?" Avalon sounded wistful and Ali touched her hand lightly.

"I'm sure of it," she said firmly. Then she added, more hesitantly, "Do you miss it? The success?"

"Yes, I miss it," Avalon admitted with a rueful grin. "I enjoyed my fame. But I don't regret the decision I made to join you. And I still have the music. Regardless of what Lissa was saying, I think that collection was the best work I've ever done and it was you who made it possible. Especially Raven—what she taught me has taken me to another level of achievement and I'm immensely grateful."

"We all owe Raven," Ali said honestly. "But she doesn't want our gratitude. She doesn't care that she's becoming a legend to us."

"Oh, I think she does care," Cloud said, entering the room with customary unconscious grace. "But Raven never asked to be turned into a myth and a pedestal isn't an easy place to stand."

On one of the back country roads of Italy, Tally had found what she was looking for. An elderly couple driving an equally ancient float-truck, a design of vehicle rarely used now that skimmers were so cheap, had stopped for them when Tally waved. In broken Italian, taught to her by Harmony, she had explained that she and her brother wanted a lift to Padua and promised that they would be no trouble. The old man had seemed doubtful, looking at their worn clothes askance. But his wife had overruled him and let the children aboard.

All they had wanted was to rest and think about the difficulties that lay ahead, but the old woman had obviously let them ride with her because she wanted someone to talk to and the twins had been an unwilling audience for her endless flood of chatter. As the float-truck wound its way up and down the rolling hills, Tally listened to what seemed like the old woman's life history. Her name was Julietta and in her long life she had accumulated enough relatives that her stories looked likely to continue throughout the entire journey: three sons and two daughters had produced nine grandchildren, the eldest of which was about to have children of her own. Tally's mind sank into a half-daze as the old lady's fluid Italian droned on telling her about Ricco and Maria and Grego and Georgiana until she couldn't remember which was which and wondered how the old lady could keep them all straight herself.

Gift's Italian was better than hers though and he seemed able to chatter back to Julietta whenever she gave him the chance to get a word in edgeways. When the old lady finally asked them about their own family it was Gift who was awake enough to think of a clever answer.

"Our parents are English, on a visit to Padua," he explained. "But Tally and I wanted to see Venice so we left them a note and begged a lift there. They'll be angry when we get back but we couldn't come to Italy and not see Venice, even if it is ruined now."

Tally couldn't understand Julietta's reply but it seemed to be something about how the English would do any crazy thing but that Venice was a grand old city, didn't she remember how it had finally been abandoned and she hoped that their parents didn't punish them too hard, although they were wicked children to run away. All of this was accompanied with chuckling laughter and Tally relaxed, realizing that Gift was doing a good job of charming this old lady. Her brother always got on with people better than she did. While Tally worried and fretted over their future, Gift's moods went from black anger to sunny good humor with an ease that she admired, although sometimes it alarmed her. Even now, while they were in greater danger than they had ever been in their lives, Gift could sit here chatting away as if he hadn't a care in the world.

Gift was asking a question of the old lady and Tally realized that she had lost track of the conversation again. It didn't seem to bother them any more than it concerned the old man. Although he seemed to have forgotten his original distrust of them he said very little, concentrating on driving the truck and staring ahead at the curving road. Suddenly Gift pinched her and Tally jolted awake, turning to him with a surprised look. He wasn't looking at her though, all his attention was on Julietta, but his hand gripped her wrist tightly and Tally tried to concentrate on the conversation.

"Greg's a good boy," Julietta was saying approvingly. "Still comes to see his old mother although he has enough work on his hands for three nowadays with his job."

"Grego's bar must have a computer terminal," Gift said cautiously and Tally stiffened, realizing what he was trying to do.

"A terminal?" Julietta snorted. "He has five, my boy. Even our old house has one. Have had for years, Maria's husband had it installed the summer they stayed with us . . ." Her voice rattled on and Gift listened politely but at the first opportunity he took up the thread of the conversation again.

"Do you think Grego would let us use a terminal when we get to Padua?" he asked. "So we can send a message to our parents to tell them where we are."

"I don't see why not," Julietta said easily. "Grego's a generous boy, always has been. He offered to buy us a new skimmer but Georgio and I don't travel as much as we used to and this old thing's always been good enough for us . . ."

She was off again and this time Gift didn't try to interrupt her. Squeezing Tally's hand he flashed her a brief smile and she smiled back. Gift had a knack for turning situations to his advantage and it looked as if meeting his friendly old lady had been a double stroke of luck. But Tally's relief didn't last for long. Now they had found a terminal they would still have to use it and Tally had no idea how they would send a message to the Hexes in England.

5

The Weight of a Talent

Alaric officially unveiled his plan that afternoon. The most senior members of the
Ghosts had gathered at the Fortress for their
regular weekly meeting. Usually not all of
them could spare time in their busy sched-
ules for more than a few words as they
passed or even make all the meetings and
briefings that were constantly being held.
Because of this Wraith had instituted the
custom of having a regular Council of War
and even Raven was expected to attend,
however busy she was.

There were eleven of them gathered
around the Council table. Anglecynn was
represented by Alaric, Geraint, Jordan and
Daniel, three of whom already knew about
the plan. The other members of the meeting
were Wraith, Kez, Ali, Luciel, Cloud,

Avalon and Raven. Typically Raven was the last to arrive and she turned up just as the others were discussing the release of Avalon's album.

Alaric decided not to speak at once. It was reassuring to wait for a while, watching the interactions between so disparate a group of people, reminding himself that they had already achieved incredibly ambitious aims. He knew that what he intended to suggest at this meeting would alarm them and disturb the fragile equilibrium they had found but he was compelled by an increasing certainty that if they didn't move soon, it would be too late.

The last few years had been almost comfortable. In evading the Seccies and stirring up trouble for the Federation the Ghosts had grown almost complacent. But Alaric knew that if they truly believed in their cause they would have to go further. They had made promises to those children they had rescued, promises of safety and freedom. Many of them were still haunted by the thought of those children they hadn't been able to rescue: mutilated at the orders of the Federation which didn't see any evil in abusing or killing Hexes. More importantly, none of the new Hexes they had discovered had Raven's skill. Whenever they asked her about it she had said only that some of the youngest children were promising and that, with her teaching, they would become more accomplished Hexes than Ali or Luciel. But they all knew the truth. No one could equal Raven and it was possible that no one ever would. That meant that the time to strike was now; before the group grew too large to hide any longer and before some accident took Raven away from them.

While Alaric had been musing, the others had still been discussing Avalon's music and he tuned in just as Wraith was mentioning the news coverage the collection had received.

"I've seen coverage on every news feed," Geraint was saying approvingly. "Most of them try to avoid any discussion of the Hex issue but some of the smaller channels have mentioned it."

"I've seen something even more interesting," Daniel added. "Ali, your father's Corporation owns Populix, doesn't it?"

"Yes," Ali replied warily. She tended to avoid anything on the vidscreen that reminded her of her father. He still thought she was dead and she had never dared to contact him, afraid he might despise her for the life she was now living.

"Well, Populix lost two reporters a couple of years ago when you were rescuing

Raven from the EF Consulate, not that she needed much rescuing." He glanced up to smile at Raven who arched an eyebrow at the comment. "The reporters died when the Seccies and the EF troops opened fire on the crowd. The channel didn't give much coverage to the event at the time, obviously they thought it wasn't worth antagonizing the government, but Populix has never been quite as sycophantic as some of the pro-Federation channels since then."

"Could that be something to do with you, Ali?" Luciel asked gently. "Perhaps your father resents the government because of what happened to you?"

"Maybe," Ali replied but she didn't look convinced.

"Anyway," Daniel continued, "Populix certainly isn't following government orders now. Although the album hasn't been banned yet all the news feeds know it's going to be so they haven't been playing it. Populix has decided differently. I didn't realize what I was seeing at first because I didn't realize Raven had released vid images along with the music—"

"You did?" Wraith interrupted him, looking at Raven and Avalon with surprise. "You didn't mention that."

"It was Cloud's idea," Avalon explained.

"But I honestly didn't think anything would come of it."

"I thought it might be interesting if Raven could depict in a visual form what she imagines the computer network to be like," Cloud explained. "Since that was what she and Avalon tried to do in words and music, I thought it would be unfortunate to leave visuals out."

"I included a set of images with the data package I posted across the net," Raven added. "Just in case."

"Well it worked!" Daniel told her. "Populix has been showing it across the clock. It's strange material but it's incredible. Cities built out of light and with rivers of color running through them. Graphically it's the best work that's ever been done—at least that's what Populix is saying."

"How can they be playing it, though?" Geraint asked. "Despite Ali's father, the Tarrell Corporation depends on the goodwill of the government and the Federation. They can't really allow one of their channels to openly oppose its wishes."

"Populix has been very careful," Daniel explained. "They regularly state that they have no interest in disseminating sedition or rebellion against the EF but they also claim that true art doesn't have an agenda and that the music and images can be appreciated without considering their content."

"But the content's what everyone's going to be thinking of, nonetheless," Luciel exclaimed triumphantly. "That's electric!"

"It gave me an idea too," Jordan added, somewhat apologetically. "I didn't mean to do anything without your consent but seeing as it's something we were doing anyway—"

"Spit it out, Jordan," Wraith said kindly. "What did you do?"

"Well, you know those tapes you and Raven gave us from the illegal laboratory? The ones with the details of the mutilations Kalden performed on the test subjects?"

"What about them?" Luciel asked. His voice was a little ragged, unsurprisingly since he had been one of the victims of those experiments.

"Well, one thing we do is regularly broadcast them to the news feeds," Jordan explained. "They never show them but we hoped if we kept sending them someone might wonder about the government coverup and if the lab was real after all. So, since Populix seemed to be going against the government, I made an anonymous call to them today and asked them if they would broadcast the tapes again."

"And?" Wraith asked eagerly.

"They said they would," Jordan replied. "Not all of them, because the subject matter was so disturbing, but they said the tapes would make an appropriate accompaniment to some of the more disturbing songs on the album and they thanked me for the suggestion."

"That's good news," Wraith said approvingly. "And it was a clever idea, Jordan. It looks as if our message might finally be getting out."

"And there's never been a better time to make a strike against the Federation," Alaric announced and everyone fell silent to look at him.

It was a moment before Alaric spoke. He knew that he had the attention of the entire council and he wanted to plead his case as well as possible. He looked around at the company as he gathered his thoughts and then, taking a deep breath, he began.

"There's never been a group like this," he said. "In all the time Anglecynn opposed Federation rule we heard of a few centers of rebellion but the Federation always found them and put them down. Until now. We've spoken of this before, of the advantages we'll have when we finally make an attempt to threaten Federation power. But we've always considered that time to be far in the future. I think that day has come now.

"It may be sooner than we expected but, if we continue as we have been, how long before the Federation decides to unleash its full force and eliminate us? If we strike a decisive blow now it may take them years to recover and those are years we can use to our advantage.

"Raven and I have discussed a plan to cripple one of the Federation's greatest assets: their communications network. We believe there's a way to either take out or take over the orbital satellite network. If we can do that the entire Federation would be reeling and then maybe we'll be able to topple it forever."

Alaric stopped speaking and Wraith took over from him.

"The Space Operations Center from which the satellite network is controlled is not one of the Federation's more heavily guarded facilities. They aren't interested in space travel and the center doesn't do much more than process information from the satellites and occasionally service them so they don't break down. Alaric has discussed with me the possibility of sending a team to Transcendence and I think the idea's a good one."

"What about the danger?" Avalon asked, voicing everyone's thoughts. "For one thing, it almost certainly couldn't be done without Raven, and we can't afford to lose her."

"You're going to, one way or the other," Raven answered her and everyone turned to look at the young Hex. She regarded them coolly in return, her onyx eyes giving them no clue to her thoughts.

Raven wasn't the thrill-seeking hacker she had been when they arrived here. She was an oasis of perfect calm in their midst, her previous rages contained by her search for the truth about Hexes. Even her wild mop of black hair had changed, tamed into a silken veil that shrouded her face as she spoke.

"I never asked for this," she told them. "It was Wraith who wanted to change the world. I've stayed for this long because I was interested but now I'm not anymore. Alaric's right when he says things have to change, and this is one of them. You need me, and I'll serve your ends while they're also mine. I'll take this fight to the Federation if that's what you want but I won't be a figurehead for a group that does nothing."

Wraith realized as he studied her that the younger sister he had persuaded to come to London with him was the only member of the group who hadn't committed herself to their cause. She had fought when she had to and they had come to rely on her but he suddenly remembered her saying: "Anyone good enough to escape the CPS isn't going to want to load themselves down with people who aren't."

"You really don't have any loyalty, do you?" Geraint asked, sounding disgusted.

"Is it loyalty to sacrifice yourself to someone else's wishes?" Raven asked and everyone realized that she hadn't answered Geraint's question. Silence fell across the room and persisted until Cloud spoke.

"I know I'm only here on sufferance, so I'll be brief," he began. "But do any of you have a right to resent Raven for this? She said she didn't ask for the role you've given her but even so she's done everything you've asked for a long time. Everything you've created here has been accomplished with her aid. Why should she watch it wither and die because you refuse to act? She's offered to strike at the Federation. Isn't that good enough?"

"No it isn't," Wraith answered him. "Because Raven's commitment to us matters more than her gifts. But it will have to do since we're not going to be offered anything else."

Avalon reached out and took his hand sympathetically. They all knew how much it hurt him that Raven was prepared to desert the group. However, they also knew that the crucial decision had been reached and, when Alaric asked for opinions on whether to attack the Space Operations Center, everyone voted in favor.

Once the vote had been taken the Council meeting moved on swiftly, all hoping to gloss over Raven's announcement.

"If we're decided that we should go to Transcendence we should discuss who'll be on the team," Wraith told them, taking charge of the meeting. "Will it be a small group or a large one? What skills are most necessary?"

"I think Raven's most qualified to judge that," Geraint replied, with a cold edge to his voice. His eyes were hard as he looked at the young Hex and asked levelly, "What would be your preference, Raven?"

"A small group," the girl replied. "Well-armed, able to respond swiftly and independently to trouble and including at least two other Hexes."

"Ali and Luciel seem the most obvious choices for that role," Wraith said. "They've been trained for the longest."

"No, not me," Ali said and, when it looked as if Wraith might be about to object, she pressed on. "I'm not really a natural Hex. I don't have the strength or the bravery. I'll help the group however I can but I don't think I'm a good choice for this mission. I don't think Raven could rely on me to come through."

"You're sure of that?" Luciel asked her seriously. "You're a lot better than you think you are, Ali."

"Maybe, but that's the important point, isn't it? I *don't* think I'm good enough and if you're honest you'll admit I'd be a liability."

"Ali has proved herself in other ways," Raven said unexpectedly. "I won't take her if she doesn't want to go."

"Very well," Wraith agreed. "What about you, Luciel?"

"I'll go," the boy replied. "I want to and, next to Raven, I'm probably the most skilled."

"What about the other Hex?" Alaric asked. "Should Avalon be the one?"

"I don't think so," Avalon replied. "I'm not good enough with weapons or computers."

"Like Ali, you have other skills," Wraith told her. "Perhaps Raven can find a second Hex among the trainees?" Raven nodded and he continued. "What about the other members of the team? I'll only ask for volunteers but I'll go myself."

"I'm not sure you should," Ali told him. "Someone has to be in charge while you're gone."

"There are enough skilled people who

can do that," Wraith assured her. "Yourself for one." The others agreed and Ali smiled, looking down at her hands. She had been worried that they would be annoyed with her for turning down the mission but instead they showed that they had enough confidence in her abilities to trust her with an equally important role.

"Geraint and I can't both go, though," Alaric said. "We have too many duties and, if you're agreeable, Gerro, I'd like to go."

"I'd like the chance to take the fight to the Feds," Geraint said. "But I think you're right and that you should go." He glanced at Raven and the others realized that he was uncomfortable with taking her orders.

"I'll go too," Jordan said and Daniel echoed her.

"Jordan perhaps," Wraith said. "But Daniel, I'm afraid you don't have the necessary skills. We'll need more experienced fighters and there's also a danger that you might be recognized."

"But I'm going," Kez said suddenly and the others realized that he had been silent for a long time. "And don't say I'm a kid. I'm one of the best marksmen you've got." Wraith hesitated but Raven replied.

"I'll take Kez," she said. "I know his capabilities."

"Then it's almost settled," Wraith concluded. "The team will consist of myself, Luciel, Alaric, Jordan and Kez. And Raven, of course."

"We still need another Hex and perhaps a couple more fighters," Alaric pointed out. "I'll ask around."

"Only volunteers, remember," Wraith reminded him. "This mission will be dangerous and I don't want to take anyone who doesn't want to come."

Halfway across Europe two children were walking into a danger they had never asked for but they didn't have any choice. Padua was not a large city by the standards of the Federation, and it was nothing in comparison with the sprawling metropolis that was Transcendence. But to Tally and Gift, who had avoided cities throughout their lives, it was alarming. Julietta, the old lady who had given them a lift, seemed perfectly comfortable as the old float-truck weaved its way through the congested roads thronged with skimmers and flitters. Padua was still mostly on one level, although on the west of the city rose about thirty corporate starscrapers, and Julietta gave her husband constant advice in how to navigate the twisting streets to Grego's bar. He gave no sign of listening to her but eventually the float-truck came to a halt in a shady avenue and a man in his thirties came out of an attractively fronted building to greet them.

Julietta started talking the moment she saw him and didn't stop until all four of them were inside the bar and seated at a table with cool drinks in front of them. Somewhere in the flood of talk the old lady had told her son who Gift and Tally were and asked him if they could use one of his computer terminals. Tally, who had been half afraid that Julietta would forget her promise, was relieved when Grego said it would be no problem at all. Gift was obviously elated that things had gone so well but Tally was almost reluctant to approach the terminal, squatting like a primitive god in the next room. She had almost no idea how to use it normally and still less of a concept of how a Hex could interact with it.

"We'll go in a minute," Gift whispered to her. "Don't worry, Tally. Look how well things are going!"

"Yeah," Tally agreed. "Maybe it's a good omen." Now wasn't the time to talk about her secret fears. After a few minutes they finished their drinks and excused themselves to go and find the terminal.

"Good luck contacting your parents,"

Grego said cheerfully. "If you can't reach them you can wait here until they're in."

"Thank you," Tally said sincerely, but when they were out of earshot she added, "We shouldn't stay though, Gift. Once we've used the terminal we should get moving. It's not safe to stay anywhere for long."

"Tally, you're paranoid," Gift said with a smile. "No one even knows we're here."

"I'm not paranoid," she protested. "Just careful." But she stopped speaking as they came face to face with the terminal.

It was on, the screen glowing with a faint light and displaying the words:

> **enter network ID password <**

Tally looked at Gift hopelessly and he shrugged.

"Touch the keypad," he suggested. "Come on, I'll do it too. Touch the keypad, close your eyes and concentrate."

"On what?" Tally asked but she followed his instructions.

"On the network," Gift said quietly. "It's there, just millimeters away. Close enough to reach out and touch."

Obediently Tally concentrated. She could hear Gift breathing softly next to her, the warmth of his hand resting next to hers on the cool terminal. She could hear Julietta's voice rising and falling in a flood of chatter in the next room and the hum of the city outside. And she could feel something else. It hovered just at the edge of her perceptions like a half-heard whisper. It was close enough to touch, a word on the tip of a tongue, an elusive memory. She tried to concentrate on it and it slipped away. Tried again, held it for a second and lost it.

"Damn," she said, instinctively opening her eyes. "I think I almost had it, then."

"Me too," Gift whispered. "Try again. Let it come naturally."

Tally closed her eyes again and tried to block out all distractions, letting her mind drift. She could feel the network but she didn't try to reach for it, allowing it to hang just beyond her reach until it seemed as if it had been there forever. Then slowly, hardly daring to breathe, she concentrated on that sensation and all of a sudden felt herself falling toward it. In her mind she was standing at a gateway and all she had to do was open a door. Reaching out more confidently she touched it and it swung open invitingly.

"Tally!" Gift exclaimed and her eyes snapped open. "Look," he said. "You did it. Look at that!"

The screen had produced a new line of text.

> **password accepted—access granted <**

"That was incredible," Tally breathed.

"What about you, did you feel it?"

"I think I did," Gift replied. "Try again. Try and enter it properly."

The twins closed their eyes again and Tally reached for the gateway in her mind. It was open now and only just out of her reach, leading into an alien world full of possibilities. Suddenly she wanted to be a part of it more than she had ever wanted anything in her life before. This was her heritage and she reached to claim it. The fall was dizzying, the gateway a black pit beneath her feet and she gasped as she fell through it and found herself flying. It was like being delirious. She had no concept of direction anymore, her mind couldn't translate what it was experiencing into the evidence of her senses. It was so much more than she had been led to believe. The network was alive, and she could feel it. A living breathing entity, not a sterile web of electronic signals and connections. She allowed herself to drift, trying to find a way of assimilating it all into her mind. Then she felt the presence of something close by and reached for it.

> ? < her mind asked, unable to formulate any more coherent thought.

> tally—? < the presence responded and excitedly Tally tried to ask a real question, holding the words in her mind and

then directing them at the presence.

>gift?—is that you/me/us/network/here/this . . . ? <

The words were jumbled up, her thoughts tangled with each other, but the response was reassuring.

> tally—difficult to think/be/imagine/dream—where/here are you/me/we? <

> somewhere/everywhere—hold on <

Tally responded, certain that if they lost track of each other they wouldn't be able to find each other again. Delicately she moved toward Gift's mind, a presence so similar in feeling to her own that she felt as if she was touching her mirror image. As she reached for him, Gift reached back for her and then they were together; their minds transmitted information to each other too quickly to be considered as words, trying to make sense of the net. They hung there for what seemed like aeons until their linked minds were able to make some sense of what surrounded them.

> a city < they thought together. > city of light/sound/movement <

It surrounded them in all directions and they regarded it with wonder, amazed that they had achieved this much. Then the urge to explore grabbed them simultaneously and their minds shared one single thought.

> let's fly <

● ● ●

The first thing Drow did when he connected to the net was to check the mail drop he had left for himself. There was no response to his message and he tried to ignore the disappointment he felt. It had been a crazy idea anyway, he told himself, sending a message to no one. But he had hoped so much, more than he had realized until this moment, that somewhere out there might be a person like himself who could understand what he felt when he was connected.

"It's too early to give up, though," he told himself firmly. "I've hardly looked properly, anyway. Just sent one message." Even as the thought came to him he felt a sudden certainty that there were people like him in the web and he knew he had to find them. Functioning on instinct alone, he let himself be pulled by the currents of the network, drawn one way then another, allowing the dataflow to take him with it. As he drifted it was clear to him that the contagion was spreading. He could feel its tendrils sliding through the network looking for a place to take hold. Whenever he neared one of those blindly grasping tentacles he changed course, not allowing it to take hold of him. He sped along the data pathways, searching for the unusual, knowing with an inexplicable certainty that he would find it.

He had left the city network long ago and as he moved out of England into the European network he could feel the black pestilence receding behind him. Rejoicing in the freedom, he coasted on the dataflow for a few moments longer then lifted above it, flying free through the network. Hurtling through the virtual world he felt something pass him and ten systems later realized there had been something strange about it. He retraced his direction and couldn't find it. Puzzled now, he engaged the mapping program he had stolen only days ago and asked it where he was. Obediently it displayed the section of the network he found himself in and a schematic of the systems he had passed through to get there. He studied the map for a while then decided it had been in the Italian section of the European net that the strangeness had found nothing. Trying to dismiss it from his mind he let himself fly and passed it again almost immediately. This time though he was prepared and he halted almost instantaneously. The strangeness did the same and they circled each other warily for a few moments before Drow reached out to it and asked.

> what are you? <

When the answer came it was a strange

mixture of personality and intellect, unmistakably human but unable to visualize itself properly, overwhelmed by the net.

> we are gift/talent—help us <

The plea instantly got Drow's attention and he moved closer.

> help how/why/who?<

> help us—gift/talent/hexes/twins— help us <

> your thoughts are not clear/understandable/precise < Drow told them, not even knowing as he thought it exactly what he meant. > can you focus? <

There was a pause as they struggled for identity and meaning and Drow realized during that space of time that the twinned minds were very young and even more inexperienced. That they called themselves Hexes frightened him with all the implications it had about his own abilities. But he was too concerned for them to worry about himself. These minds were lost in the net and beginning to panic.

> help us < they pleaded. > you are like us/with us/part of us—help us <

Realizing that he wasn't going to get any more sense out of them like this, Drow engaged his mapping program again and extended it toward the strangers.

> where did you come from? < he asked them, trying to make the question as firm as

he could. **> show me <**

For a while there was a silence, then the minds reached back to him, handing him his own map with a location marked on it.

> *here* <

Reaching for the minds of the strangers, Drow enfolded them with his own and was overcome by confusion like a blow. They were mixed up in each other and in the net, rapidly losing their sanity in trying to assimilate too much at once. Imagining himself as pulling them behind him, Drow began to travel through the net and slowly they followed. He didn't dare move too fast in case he lost them, and the journey back to the location they had marked seemed to take forever. All the while their minds cried out to him to help them until his own head rang with the plea. Eventually the mapping program signaled to him that he had reached his destination and he released his hold on the minds.

> leave now < he told them. **> return/let go/detach <**

> how? < they asked him in confusion and he attempted to show them, filling his mind with his own experience of the network, of how he entered and left it. Then abruptly they were gone and Drow found himself alone in a small private system.

> system identity < he demanded and

the amateur security precautions melted away to inform him where he was.

> **system licensed to Gregori Vecci— Padua—Italy Europe <**

Drow had no idea what that indicated about the identity of the two children he had rescued but he intended to find out. Reaching toward the only terminal in use on the system he told it what words to display.

> **gift/talent—can you understand me? <**

6

Power to Shut Heaven

Gift shook his head to clear it and stared blankly at the computer terminal in front of him, trying to figure out what had happened. He had to remember who he was. It seemed as if he had been Gift-Talent for a hundred years, so long that he couldn't think straight as an individual, but the wall chronometer informed him that only five minutes had passed since they had attempted to make contact with the terminal. Remembering that he was Gift reminded him to look for Tally. She was lying on the floor beside the terminal and he bent to shake her lightly.

"Tally, Tally?" he said, checking her pulse. It was beating quickly but steadily and his sister's eyes blinked open, wide with fright.

"Gift?" she said hesitantly.

"Yes, it's me. And you're Tally," he said with a quick laugh. "Can you remember that?"

"I can now," Tally said, sitting up carefully. "What happened?"

"I suspect the answer's on the disk," Gift replied. "But it's not difficult to guess. We're not experienced enough with this. But I think we met someone in there who was."

"Yes." Tally stood up too quickly and then swayed with a momentary dizziness. Gift reached to support her and then froze.

"Tally, look!" he said eagerly. The message on the terminal had changed. Now it read:

>gift/talent—can you understand me?<

The twins stared at the terminal together and they turned to look at each other with wide grins.

"We found them!" Gift exclaimed. "It actually worked."

"Maybe," Tally was more cautious. "We don't know who this is, yet."

"Then let's find out," Gift replied and reached for the terminal, searching for letters on the keypad that would enable him to form a response. Slowly he inputted the words:

> This is Gift. Who are you?<

> My name is Drow. < came the reply instantly. > Are you all right, Gift? Is Talent all right? <

Tally moved toward the keyboard and Gift pointed out the keys to type with. She composed her own message even more slowly, taking time about what she wanted to say. Gift could barely contain his impatience; he was so elated that he was almost dancing on the spot.

> This is Talent. I am fine. I think we may owe you our lives. Thank you. <

> It was my pleasure. < the stranger reassured them. > But I don't know how I did it. I'm not much more experienced than you with this. What did you mean when you said you were Hexes? <

Tally glanced at Gift and he frowned, then shrugged, reaching for the terminal to type.

> This is Gift. Tally and I are both Hexes. Our lives are in danger because of it and we need your help. You must be a Hex too or you couldn't exist in the network this way. Please help us. <

It took Gift a long time to finish his message but this time the response was not instantaneous. The twins waited anxiously and then gradually the words appeared on the screen.

> You know much more than I do, I

think. I've used computers all my life but I never realized that this ability made me a Hex. I could never understand it. I didn't know what being a Hex meant. Now it makes sense. I want to know more but what you want is more important, right now. How are you in danger? How can I help? <

Tally breathed a huge sigh of relief and clung to Gift.

"Thank God!" she said. "He'll help us." But then her natural wariness returned and she said with a troubled look, "How *can* he help us? What should we ask for?"

"This was *your* idea," Gift reminded her.

"I never thought it would work though," she replied. "I never imagined—"

"Well, let's tell him about our problem then," Gift interrupted her. "Maybe he'll have an idea of what to do." Reaching for the keypad he replied:

> We are in Italy in a city called Padua. We are being hunted by the Security Services and Federation Troops. We are trying to contact a group of Hexes in England. A Hex escaped from Federation custody there. We thought that person could help us. Is that you?<

>No, it's not. I'm sorry. <

The answer came back slowly and Gift felt sure that the person they were speaking to was thinking hard about what they were saying.

> But perhaps I can help you find them. First tell me though how urgently you need help. Are you safe where you are? <

> For the time being. < Gift replied. > But we can't stay where we are for long. <

There was a long pause and then a long answer began to reel itself on to the screen and Gift and Tally leaned forward so as not to miss any of it.

> Even a small city has crime. Padua must have some gangers somewhere. Find them. Gangers mean fixers and fixers will do anything for creds. Find a fixer and give them this call-code: Eu/Lon-node/Bethnel/chr#34850. Say I will pay money for them to find a safe place to hide you. Ask for a room with a terminal and then call me again from there. Don't say anything to the fixer about being Hexes. Don't say anything about the Seccies or the Feds. Just ask for a room and offer the money. Look confident enough and they will agree. Do you understand?<

>Yes. Thank you. < Tally responded. > How much will it cost you? I am sorry to cause you trouble. <

>Don't worry. < Drow replied. > I'm a hacker. I can find the creds. I will do my

best to help you. Go now and find a safe place. Write down the call-code. Don't lose it.<

>We won't. Thank you. < Tally replied while Gift fumbled in their bag for something to write on. As he scribbled down the code Tally keyed in one last message.

> We owe you everything. <

Drow stared at his terminal screen but nothing more was added. He had dropped back through the net after making the connection with the Italian system and had watched with fascination as the strangers he met in the net explained their problem to him. Stunned by the revelation that he was a Hex he had hardly been able to think straight but he had suggested the only idea that occurred to him and hoped desperately he had told them the right thing to do. Now their last words hung on the screen.

> We owe you everything. <

He had no idea what to do now. Talent and Gift had been searching the net for a savior and had found him. Now he would have to take on their search himself. He needed to find a Hex and he had no idea how to do it. With a sigh he turned off the terminal and went to find his father. Maybe he would have an idea. Drow had no doubt that his family would accept the knowledge that he was a Hex with equanimity. They cared nothing for Federation laws and restrictions, and the injunction against mutants was no more than a Federation law. He hurried down the stairs into the main room and came face to face with the net.

It hung on the vidscreen in the room. The same vision of the net that he saw from his terminal. The vision he had never been able to describe to anyone.

"That's it!" he exclaimed. "That's what I see."

Electra and Innuru were sitting in front of the vidscreen and they both turned around at his words, their expressions alarmed.

"Drow—" Electra began but her words were cut off abruptly as the images on the screen changed and Drow took a step backward instinctively.

In his worst nightmares he could never have imagined a horror like this. The city of light that had hung tantalizingly on the screen was replaced with a room that seemed a bizarre cross between a high-tech laboratory and a medieval torture chamber. A small childish figure lay enclosed in instruments, writhing in silent agony as a group of white-coated scientists stood around making notes. A list of statistics scrolled past on the screen. Details of experiments that made Drow's throat contract with nausea and finally a death date. It hung on the screen for a second, superimposed over the face of the mutilated child. Then the image was replaced by another scene, almost identical except that this child was younger still. Incongruously, music was playing in the background. A haunting twisted guitar sound that burned into his brain like a wire.

"Turn it off," he gasped, reaching for the control. But Innuru got there first and the vidscreen faded into blackness. Even with it off the images still played in Drow's mind and he stared at the blank screen transfixed.

It wasn't until Innuru shook him hard that Drow realized his sister and her husband had moved and were standing on either side of him, looking into his eyes with anxious expressions.

"Drow, are you all right?" Electra was shaking.

"I think so," he said shakily. "What was that?"

"The end of Populix as a news channel," Innuru said grimly. "That stuff's going to get them taken off the air for sure."

Drow looked at him blankly and Electra explained further.

"It was a program about the new release from Avalon. The rock singer who went underground? A collection of music was released on the net claiming to be by her and Populix is the only channel playing it. The city images were also released by the terrorists Avalon's supposed to have joined but the torture stuff comes off the news feeds. Four years back that stuff was released about experiments on Hex kids. But the government denied it all."

"Looks like some people didn't believe them," Innuru pointed out and Electra nodded.

"Do you believe them?" Drow asked. "Did that . . . were those images real kids, or not?"

Innuru and Electra looked at each other and then Innuru took charge.

"Sit down, Drow," he ordered, leading him to the battered sofa. "I want to ask a question first. When you said that the city was what you saw, did you mean what I think?"

"You mean am I a Hex, don't you?" Drow said slowly. He studied Innuru's face but could find no clue to what his brother-in-law was thinking. For the first time he wondered if it was wise to reveal his secret. But Electra and Innuru were family and, suddenly remembering Tally and Gift and how desperately they needed help, he knew he couldn't wait to be certain. If he couldn't trust Innuru, who could he trust?

"That's what I'm asking," Innuru agreed, waiting for his answer and Drow bowed his head.

"Yes," he said quietly. "I think I am."

"That's what I thought," Innuru replied and turned to Electra. "Get the rest of the family," he said. "Your father and your sisters."

Without a word Electra left the room and Innuru turned back to Drow. Drow looked back at him with wide scared eyes, uncertain of what to say and, when Innuru smiled, his relief was enormous.

"No Chrome should be ashamed to be a Hex," the older ganger told him. "Hexes have a genetic gift for the skills the rest of us have to teach ourselves." He touched Drow's shoulder lightly. "Don't worry, Drow. The family has talked about this before. You're not the first Chrome this has happened to."

"And not the last either," a strong voice came from behind them and Drow turned around to see his father. "Don't you start getting scared of the Seccies or the other Federation lap-dogs now. There's no one in this family who wouldn't hide you from them and, if we can't do it, there are others even better at it."

"Do you mean the terrorists?" Drow asked, his mind working quickly. "The ones Electra said Avalon's with. The ones who released the music?"

His father came across to sit beside him and his sisters gathered around the sofa to hear his explanation. But it was Innuru who spoke first.

"First thing you gotta know is that we don't talk about it," he said. "Not ever."

"That is important," Drow's father agreed. "Half the city's looking for the people who blew up half the Federation Consulate to rescue one of their own and if the Seccies found them—"

"The people who blew up the Consulate?" Drow interrupted suddenly. "They must be the ones I'm looking for!"

"Looking for them?" His father frowned. "Why? Surely you know you're safe here?"

"Yes, of course." A rush of relief flooded through Drow as he properly understood that for the first time. His family was as trustworthy as he had always thought they would be. But the realization made it all the more urgent to help Gift and Tally. They had no one to rely on except for him.

"It's not for me, I'm looking for them," Drow began to explain. "It's for someone else, two kids in Italy."

"In Italy?" Electra asked, puzzled and Drow continued quickly.

"They contacted me through the net," he said. "At least we met each other there. It was kind of an accident that they found me. But they were looking for other Hexes. Their names are Gift and Talent and they're very young but they're on the run from the Federation. It sounds like everyone's hunting them and they badly need help. I promised I'd try and find Hexes in England for them. There's supposed to be a group that can help and it must be these terrorists. I'm certain of it."

Tally clutched the precious call-code, scribbled on a piece of sandwich wrapper, tightly in her hand all the time while Gift talked to Julietta. He admired the fluid way her brother lied to the old lady, assuring her that they had contacted their parents and were on the way to meet them. He thanked her and Grego politely for their help as if he had nothing to worry about. No one could possibly have guessed from his behavior that he had been trapped inside the computer network less than ten minutes earlier. At that thought Tally had to repress her hysteria. Of course no one could guess that, she thought. It's insanity.

She attempted to smile her own good-
byes as Gift took her hand and led her out
of the bar but she was still shaking inside
and her brother knew it. As soon as they
were outside he set a brisk pace down the
street, talking to her confidently.

"It's all right, Tally, really," he said.
"We're both OK and Drow's going to help
us. He already has. All we need to do is find
the kind of people that Seccies think of as
criminals." He squeezed her hand tightly as
he added, "Now don't worry about that
either. I know what you're like. But just
because the Seccies think gangers are criminals doesn't mean that they're people we
wouldn't want to meet. And it won't be difficult to find them, either. Look at us," he
gestured down at their tattered and dirty
clothes. "We'll fit right in, just look for people like us."

"People like us," Tally replied dazedly.
But the soothing flow of Gift's words *was*
relaxing her. She didn't feel as worried
when he was so confident that Drow's
advice would help them. Tally didn't know
whether to be thrilled that they had actually
succeeded in contacting someone or
despairing that they had not found the people they were looking for. But she was
beginning to recover from the shock of
being trapped in the data network and

Gift's words were slowly penetrating her mind.

"Yes, like us," Gift replied, continuing to speak soothingly. "I'm sure it won't be difficult—"

"Beggars," Tally said abruptly and he frowned, turning to face her.

"What was that?" he asked.

"Beggars," she said again, her mind slowly beginning to work again. "That's what we look like."

"And beggars are street people who might know where we can find a fixer," Gift replied. "Or at least know someone who knows." He grinned. "Tally, you're brilliant. Even when you look as vacant as a blank wall you still come up with the goods." He hugged her impulsively and Tally hugged him back, smiling.

"We should find the city center," she pointed out. "Beggars approach tourists and there are always more tourists in the center of town."

"Good idea," Gift agreed and they looked around for signs. Tally was the first to spot what they wanted.

"Look!" she said, pointing to a sign which read *Centro Historico.* "That looks promising."

"Come on then," Gift said, heading for it. "What are we waiting for?"

● ● ●

It took Drow a while to convince his family how urgently Gift and Tally needed help. But, once he had told his story a second time, answering their questions as best he could, Innuru and his father got a look of determination.

"All right then," his father said. "We'll have to make contact with the Hexes here and tell them that two of their own need their help. But someone will have to stay ready in case any Italian fixer calls that code and asks for money. Electra, that's something you can do." He looked around at the others, considering for a moment. "Selver, you watch the news feeds while we're gone. Keep up with what's happening. I have a feeling that this story of Populix's is going to stir things up. And Arachne, you go and find us transportation. We've got a trip to make."

"A trip where?" Drow asked. "To see these Hexes?"

"Unfortunately not," his father replied. "All we have is one contact. A fixer who they trust. But if we can persuade her it's urgent enough she may tell us how to find them."

Drow waited impatiently while Arachne went to borrow a flitter from another gang member and Innuru carefully checked through his weaponry. Unusually he collected a snub-nosed blaster and handed it to Drow.

"Best to have some protection," he said.

Drow glanced at his father but, when he made no objection, he hoisted the weapon carefully, feeling its weight.

"Thanks, Innuru," he said gratefully. Despite the fact that he had wandered the city without weapons many times, he was starting to feel an irrational fear that this time the Seccies would pick him up and know him for a Hex.

"Be careful with it," his brother-in-law warned him. "Don't use it unless you have to."

It was then that Arachne returned with the news that a flitter was waiting outside and Drow hastily got to his feet.

It was early evening outside, the streets still filled with hawkers and visitors coming into Chrome territory to do business with the legitimate traders. But with the approach of night more gangers were out on the streets too, ready to do a different kind of business. A Chrome patrol loitered in the plaza nearby, watching passers-by with a studied casualness. The little light that filtered down from the upper levels of the city during the middle of the day had been extinguished and across the ganglands the artificial lighting had been intensified so that Drow felt as if he was walking in a black and white landscape: the brilliant pools of light intensifying the shadows around them. He shuddered as he remembered the images he had seen on the vidscreen. Horrors could live in the light as easily as trust could lie in the shadows, he reminded himself. As he climbed into the back of the little flitter that stood waiting, he found himself thinking of the levels controlled by the Ghosts. The throng of people moving through Chrome territory now was a vivid contrast to the eerie emptiness of the Ghost levels, brightly lit even when no one walked their streets. For the first time he wondered if that was deliberate. So little was known about the Ghosts that anyone who passed through their territory would have to guess as to their intentions. All those lights and surveillance equipment were impressive but they were made all the more intimidating because a passer-by had no face to put them to. Here the Chromes made a show of force but the Ghosts kept their force hidden and were respected for it.

Drow realized that the elusive gang had been more intelligent in their use of the areas they controlled than he had realized and he felt a sudden curiosity about what so much secrecy was designed to conceal. If

Rhiannon Lassiter

the revelation hadn't come just as he was thinking about the Hexes he might not have made a connection. But as it was a sudden certainty hit him and he almost spoke it aloud. Then he stopped himself. It was possible that the Ghosts hid the Hexes within their midst but there was no reason to assume that made it true. For now he would hold on to his suspicions until he had met his contact of his father's. Hopefully that would shed more light on the situation and perhaps prove or disprove his ideas.

It had taken Cloud some time to find Raven. After the discussion of the attack on Transcendence she had disappeared and his enquiries had discovered no trace of her. Although the others at the meeting were divided between anger and hurt at her announcement, not one of them had attempted to confront her. Ali had told him outright that she wouldn't dare and Luciel and Kez appeared to feel the same way. Avalon had obviously decided it wasn't really her business to speak to Raven and had turned her attention to trying to talk to Wraith, who was more than usually silent. Cloud didn't envy her that task. The white-haired ganger was someone that *he* found intimidating and he hadn't tried to broach

134

the subject of Raven with him. Alaric was likewise absorbed in trying to calm down Geraint, who saw Raven's behavior as an outright betrayal. Lots of ruffled feathers was Cloud's own verdict on the situation. But although the group's behavior made an interesting social study it didn't help him in tracking down the person who had started it all off.

Ironically, it wasn't until he had abandoned the search that he found her. The larger of the Ghost enclaves contained an old vidplex building: a series of large vidscreens which had once been open to the public. Now it was mostly disused, although the group had held some of their larger meetings there. However, the screens were still connected and Cloud had wandered inside with the vague intention of trying to pick up a news feed on one of them. When he reached the building he realized that it wasn't completely deserted. The long hallways echoed with the sound of his footsteps but in the distance he could hear the sound of music and, following it, he came to the hall which held the largest of the five screens. The double doors slid open as he approached and for a moment he was blinded by the light from the screen, filling the darkened room. He recognized the vid playing instantly—he had designed most of it, a sequence to accompany Masque's last release. It had been called "Transformations" and its images of dark passages filled with shadows had been Raven's first clue that Avalon was a Hex.

Cloud walked down the ranks of seating to where a figure sat at dead center of the first row. Raven didn't look at him, her black eyes focused on the screen, but as he sat down she asked:

"How long have you been looking for me?"

"A few hours," Cloud replied. "But now I've given up, I have a feeling you don't want to be found."

"Maybe I just don't want the search to be easy," Raven said, glancing sideways at him with a half smile. "Why were you looking for me?"

"Curiosity perhaps," Cloud told her. "Why did you tell the others you wouldn't stay with them unless they faced the Federation?"

"Why do you think I did?" Raven asked him and he studied her carefully before answering.

"I wondered if you did have any intention of leaving," he said. "You knew that their reaction would be to agree with you. They hadn't any other choice. So, did you really intend to leave?"

For a few moments Raven was silent, watching the darkness unfold on the screen in front of her. Then she said softly, "I always mean what I say."

"So if they'd called your bluff you'd have left?" Cloud asked her.

"It wasn't a bluff," Raven said sharply. She swung around in her seat to regard him seriously. "But there doesn't always have to be a plan. If I leave, I can find my own future." She laughed briefly. "Sometimes, the way they rely on me here, I wonder if it makes much difference with or without them."

"Would you go up against the Federation on your own?" Cloud asked quickly. "Without the support of the Ghosts?"

Raven smiled secretively, moving her head slightly so that her long curtain of hair swung forward, obscuring his view of her.

"Cloud," she said quietly. "Every breath I take on this Earth is a strike against the Federation. My entire life is a terrorist action. The only way for me to stop fighting them would be to stop living. Does it matter very much how or where I do it?"

"Yes," said Cloud. "To quote your brother: yes, it does."

"Why?"

"Because danger isn't consistent," he said with an edge in his voice. "Hasn't

Avalon increased her danger by joining this group, despite the fact that she was always a Hex?"

"She's put herself less at risk by learning how to use her abilities," Raven pointed out.

"Point taken," Cloud granted. "But tell me honestly, how much would the danger to you increase when you move against the heart of Federation power?"

"Exponentially," Raven replied. "As it does every day."

"How?"

"Because," Raven said slowly, "somewhere, not so very far away, a group of bureaucrats sit in a room being berated by a government official who can't believe that after four years they are still no closer to catching me and wiping the rest of the Hexes off the face of the Earth."

"How do you know?" Cloud asked.

"Because that's the way the world works," Raven replied. "Until we change it."

7

The Keys of Hell

Arachne piloted the little flitter skillfully through the city. The weaving course she took was as much to avoid rival gangs as the Seccies or other law enforcement agencies. The flitter was unmarked but all four of them were wearing Chrome colors and the silver metal threaded into their braids would have identified them even without that. Drow looked around curiously at the course Arachne took. His practiced eyes could tell that she was being extra careful. She didn't pass through any territories controlled by gangs with which the Chromes had even minor disputes, keeping to friendly or neutral ganglands despite the erratic path it meant she had to fly. But he was surprised when she finally brought the flitter to the ground in the center of Snake territory.

The Snakes were a gang with which the Chromes had almost no contact at all. They were a minor, if respected, clan. Although they were loyal to each other as a group they had diverse interests and were often found hiring themselves out to other gangs as mercenaries. But, despite their lack of unity, Drow had never heard anyone disparage the Snakes' firepower and he felt nervous as a large man dressed in battered combats appeared from the side of a building to block the end of a narrow spur of walkway ahead of them. The walkway was the only route to a section of building with metal-shielded windows all the way up to the next level. The unknown ganger didn't move out of the way as they approached. Instead he leveled a heavy assault rifle at them and said slowly:

"That's close enough."

"We don't want trouble," Innuru said, speaking for all of them. "We just want to see your fixer."

The man looked Innuru up and down, then turned his attention to the rest of them.

"Chromes, aren't you?" he said. "Don't you have any fixers of your own back in hacker town?"

"They don't have the information we need," Drow's father said, meeting the big man's eyes. "The Countess does."

"The Countess doesn't take on much work nowadays," the man told him. "What makes you think she'll want to see you?"

"She's seen Chromes before," Drow's father continued. "And it is important."

The man considered them for a while longer; then eventually he nodded.

"Reckon it must be," he said. "You're not the usual types we get around here." He stepped back a little to let them past. "You can go in," he continued. "But walk softly or you'll get more than you bargain for."

The four of them trooped across the narrow spur of walkway to the entrance to the building. The main door stood open and they stepped through into a wide hall. Inside, two gangers in Snake colors, their hair dyed a distinctive dark blue, loitered near an impressively high-tech flitter. Another three people stood on the other side of the hall, guarding the only door which was not blocked up with rubble. The Snake gangers ignored them as Drow and his family crossed the hall to approach the door guards. They were only a few meters away when one of the guards, a blonde woman, gestured toward a gleaming vidcom unit to her right.

"State your names and business into the vidcom," she said. "The Countess herself will decide if she wishes to see you."

As his father moved toward the unit, Drow looked around thoughtfully. The building was undecorated and the doors blocked up with rubble gave the impression of dilapidation. But the flitter looked custom-designed, built for speed and power, and the vidcom unit was a recent model from a specialty computer hardware company. He wondered how much of the apparent disrepair of this building was intentional.

"My name is Mohan," his father was saying. "With me are my son-in-law Innuru and my children: Arachne and Drow. We believe we have information of interest to some contacts of yours." He glanced at the guards. "Contacts who guard their privacy seriously."

They waited for a few moments in silence until a dry voice spoke out of the vidcom unit.

"All my associates guard their privacy seriously," it said. "Or else I would not do business with them. I hope that you will show a similar discretion. Leave your weapons and approach the stairway."

The guards looked at them expectantly and Drow's father stepped forward to divest himself of this blaster and two knives. Innuru and Arachne followed suit and Drow handed over his blaster after them. However, the guards did not move away from the door and when Innuru attempted to pass them the blonde woman raised a hand in warning.

"*All* your weapons," she said. "Including those stealth pistols."

Innuru and Drow's father exchanged looks. Then they each reached down to produce a slim lightweight pistol from their boots. Drow blinked in surprise. The pistols had an iridescent sheen, showing that they had been coated in a material intended to baffle scanning devices. But despite this protection the Countess' guards had still spotted them, and he wondered what kind of security system this fixer had that would make that possible.

Once the pistols had been surrendered the guards moved away from the door and it slid open to allow their group to enter. They found themselves standing at the bottom of a wide sweeping staircase and were almost immediately confronted with multiple images of themselves. Every surface in all directions was made of reflective shielding, strong enough to withstand a bomb blast as far as Drow could tell. He was certain that there was enough equipment behind the walls to scan every inch of their bodies and probably tell the Countess what they had eaten for breakfast if she wanted to know. It made him nervous to head up those stairs, conscious that he was under invisible observation. Traveling through the Ghost territory had been unnerving enough but at least then he had seen the surveillance equipment. Here he knew it existed but there was no sign to confirm his suspicions.

"Hell of a set up," Innuru muttered to himself and Arachne smiled.

"Come on, Inni," she pointed out. "At least it lets us know we're dealing with talent, yeh?"

"Talent and quality," Drow's father agreed. "And, since the lady is almost certainly listening, she may as well know she has all our admiration."

That silenced them for a while and they climbed the rest of the stairs quickly. At the summit they found themselves standing on a narrow landing and facing a plain mirrored wall. Drow glanced at the others quizzically and Innuru shrugged. As he did so the wall slid out of the way and they saw a room full of screens and terminals behind it. All of them relaxed imperceptibly at the sight. Up until now the fixer's base had been alien territory but this room was much like any building controlled by Chromes. It was unmistakably the property of a computer fanatic. The cases and crates of equipment stacked against the walls were the latest in tech and the plainly dressed woman standing at the center of the room had the typical casual arrogance of a hacker. She had short shaved dark hair and wore black coveralls. Her only other adornment were the multiple bands that circled her arms, covered with controls and mini-screens.

The fixer didn't bother with greetings but launched straight into the matter of their business.

"You say you have information for my contacts," she said sharply. "But I doubt you bring it as a gift."

Drow's father opened his mouth to speak but Drow interrupted him. It was he who was the cause of their contacting this woman and he didn't want to hide behind his family when the responsibility should be his.

"It's strange you should say that," he said. "For it's a gift and a talent that we bring you."

Innuru looked at him sharply but didn't stop him from speaking and his father rested his hand on Drow's shoulder in silent support.

"A gift and a talent," the fixer mused, then smiled suddenly. "I like you, boy," she said. "You have a way with words. But speak to me openly. Which of my contacts is it that you truly seek?"

"We're looking for Hexes," Drow said boldly. "And my father gave me to understand you have a connection with them."

"It's known to certain of our gang," his father explained. "In the past when children have been at risk from the CPS you were a contact between us and those who were able to hide them. I come to you on behalf of my son, who may need the help of these people. But his concern is for friends of his who need it even more."

"Such altruism," the Countess said. "But it seems that your kind are increasingly supporting each other, boy. So my connections may help you. Though I make no promises."

"Then you do know the Hexes?" Drow asked eagerly. "Will you put us in touch with them? That's all I ask."

"I shall endeavor to," the Countess replied.

"We will of course pay a finder's fee," Drow's father added but the Countess shook her head.

"It's not necessary in this case," she replied. "Those who you seek are generous with their resources, especially when I can pass them news of their own. One moment and we shall see if they will meet with you."

She walked over to one of the many terminals that lined the walls and spoke to it, the unit responding perfectly to her voice commands.

"Dragon's Nest," she told it and the screen sprang to life, revealing a young girl with brown hair and a serious expression.

"Dragon's Nest," she said immediately. *"What can I do for you, Countess?"*

"It's a question of what I may do for you," the Countess replied. Then she turned to Drow and beckoned him toward her. "I have one of your people here, anxious for help," she said.

The girl on the screen looked at Drow and her blue-green eyes flickered for a second in what looked like surprise. But her voice was level as she asked, *"How may I help you then?"*

"My name is Drow," he said hesitantly. "I'm a hacker and, I think, a Hex as well. I'd like to meet you, to learn more about you. But first I urgently need your help. I have friends, two kids, who are in danger from the Federation. They're Hexes although they don't know much about how to use the net and they told me that Hexes in England might be able to save them. If you can help—"

"Naturally we will help as much as we can," the girl said and smiled quickly. *"But I don't have the authority to say how. You'll have to*

speak to my superiors. Probably with the Raven herself."

"The Raven?" Drow asked, looking up at the Countess for clarification.

"Raven brought down the CPS laboratory that performed experiments on your kind," the fixer explained. "She escaped EF custody and it's her skills that have helped the Hexes become ghosts on the net."

"Ghosts!" Drow exclaimed. "Are you the Ghosts?" He looked eagerly at the girl on the screen. "I was almost certain of it," he confessed. "Will you let me come to you and explain?"

The girl hesitated for a moment then said, *"One minute, while I confirm."*

The screen went black and Drow turned to his father with a smile.

"They *will* help," he said with relief. "I'm sure they can."

His father nodded but had no time to say anything else as the screen brightened again and the girl's face reappeared.

"You may meet with us," she said. *"Countess, are Finn and Jeeva still with you?"*

"Downstairs," the fixer confirmed. "Shall I send this boy with them?"

"If you would," the girl nodded.

Innuru looked doubtful and frowned at the Countess.

"Drow shouldn't go alone," he said.

"Ask if his family may come with him."

"Innuru," Drow turned his face to his brother-in-law, "there's no need. This is my trouble and my concern. I trust these people. To help me and to help Gift and Tally. I don't mind going alone."

"Then we'll expect you shortly," the girl on the screen said and her image blanked out abruptly.

"Don't be concerned," the Countess said seriously. "Drow has nothing to fear."

Innuru still looked uncertain but Drow's father nodded and hugged his son quickly.

"You will be safe with these people," he said. "We've trusted our children to them before and what news we have reports them safe and well. That these Hexes can offer such security when they are being hunted as the Federation has never hunted anyone before shows that they are trustworthy."

"Take care of yourself, Drow," Arachne said quietly.

"And contact us as soon as you can," Innuru added.

Drow nodded, almost too excited to speak. But he looked at all of them, soaking in the sight in case he didn't see them again for a long time.

● ● ●

The twins waited anxiously outside the crumbling warehouse. It had taken all Gift's powers of persuasion to convince the Italian kids they had found begging from tourists to tell them where they might find gangers and when they had reached this unprepossessing building a surly young boy had told them only to wait while he went inside.

"Look at it this way," Gift said positively. "We have got this far. It looks like our luck might have started to change."

Tally nodded but didn't say anything. Now that she had recovered from the shock of her experience in the net her mind was racing. Gift was right to say they had done well to achieve as much as they had but she was trying to concentrate on the steps ahead. Her musings were interrupted by the reappearance of the boy who had told them to wait.

"You're go to inside," he said in thickly accented Italian, jerking his thumb at the warehouse. "Rosso will meet with you."

The twins got to their feet slowly, hoisting their battered pack between them and headed toward the door. The boy watched them expressionlessly as they entered the darkened building. Inside, the warehouse had been divided into low-rent accommodation. Flimsy-looking partition walls had been put up around the sides of the warehouse space and a rusty metal stairway led up to a second floor which was similarly divided. A group of people were clustered around a kind of seating area near the bottom of the metal steps. Torn sofas and chairs had been pulled into a rough semi-circle facing an antique vidscreen. As Gift and Tally approached, squinting in the poor light, a teenager with reddish hair signaled to them to come closer. They did so reluctantly. There were about nine young people watching the screen and all of them looked confident and relaxed despite the shoddy surroundings. Gift was the first to speak as they reached the seating area.

"Are you Rosso?" he asked in careful Italian.

"I am," the red-headed boy said with a penetrating stare. "And who are you?"

"I'm Gift and this is my sister, Tally," Gift explained. "We need somewhere to stay for a couple of days. We can pay."

"Just as well," Rosso said with a short laugh. "Otherwise we wouldn't be talking. How much cred you got?"

"Nothing with us," Gift admitted. "But we have a friend who can send you the creds by data transfer and we can pay extra for the inconvenience."

"Maybe," Rosso looked thoughtful.

"What have kids like you got to be hiding from anyway?"

"We have a couple of convictions for theft," Gift lied smoothly. "And if the Seccies catch us we'll end up being made wards of the state. We're orphans and they'll put us in a blockhouse if we're caught."

"Yeah?" Rosso didn't look entirely convinced but something on the vidscreen had caught his attention: a sports match was beginning and the other teenagers were turning up the sound on the ancient unit. "All right then," he said quickly. "Give me your friend's call-code and take room sixteen for now. That suit you?"

"That's great," Gift said thankfully. "Thank you."

"No problem," Rosso replied, already turning away to look at the screen.

Room sixteen turned out to be a small windowless room on the second floor. Through the flimsy partition walls they could hear the sounds of the vidscreen even from this distance and sounds of conversations and arguments coming from nearby rooms. There were three stained mattresses lying on the floor and a heap of equally dirty blankets piled up in the corner of the room.

"Doesn't seem like much of a palazzo,

does it?" Gift said with a half smile.

"I'm more concerned that the door doesn't lock," Tally replied and her brother looked frustrated.

"What are you worrying about now?" he asked. "That lot downstairs couldn't care less about us. And Drow's plan worked fine."

"I suppose so." Tally said. She sat down on the edge of one of the mattresses, uncertainly. "But if they knew who we were we'd be in real trouble. I just don't feel safe here, that's all."

"You never feel safe anywhere, Tally," Gift pointed out. "Come on, I've got a deck of cards somewhere in my pack. Let's play a game or something. It'll take your mind off it."

"All right," Tally agreed. "I suppose there's not much else to do."

Outside the door to room sixteen an Italian teenager leaned on the rail that overlooked the next level with a thoughtful expression. Rosso hadn't cared that the two kids were telling an obvious lie but he'd gone upstairs after them to fetch a crate of alcohol from his own room and overheard Tally's remark. Now the crate lay forgotten beside him as he considered what to do. His gang was about as low as they came in Padua's hierarchy and right now they could barely afford to eat, let alone buy alcohol or repair the increasingly unreliable vidscreen. If by chance the two kids were important to someone there might be a chance for him to make money from it. Slowly he picked up the crate of beer and carried it downstairs, dumping it by the rotting sofas.

"I've got to go and make a call," he told his friends. "I'll be back in a moment."

None of them paid him much attention, although one started to hand out drinks. Shrugging, Rosso wandered toward the door of the warehouse. He didn't own a vidcom and would have to use a public one in town. But, before he called the kids' friend to arrange money, he'd contact a friend he hadn't seen for a while. Nikki wasn't much of a friend, never using his position in the local Seccie force to help Rosso, but he did sometimes pay for information and these kids might be worth something to him.

Raven and Cloud wandered out of the vidplex slowly with no particular plan of where to go next. Raven had spoken vaguely of checking up on Charis, the Hex they'd recently rescued, to give her an initial evaluation. But they had only reached the end of the street when a figure rushed out of a nearby building and raced up to them. It was Maggie, one of the Anglecynn members, and Raven and Cloud paused to wait for her.

"Raven!" she said breathlessly, as she reached them. "People have been looking for you. An emergency meeting's been called at the Fortress and they want you to be there."

"Who does?" Raven asked sharply. "And who called this meeting?"

"I've no idea," Maggie said blankly. "I thought you might know what it was about. But I think Alaric and Jordan are there."

"What kind of emergency is it?" Cloud asked. "The kind where everyone has to assume battle stations and prepare for serious trouble or the kind that's called because people have nothing better to do with their time?"

"How should I know?" Maggie said again, then she gave Cloud a suspicious look. "But speaking of having nothing to do, why doesn't anyone ever see *you* working?"

"Perhaps because my work is too important for you to know about," Cloud replied mischievously.

Raven shook her head at him. "We don't

have time for this," she said. "Cloud, pull in your claws and find me a flitter so we can find out how urgent this emergency is."

It took them half an hour to reach the Fortress and Raven was distracted most of the time, concentrating her attention on piloting the flitter. She didn't travel as fast as she could, to Cloud's relief, obviously trusting that whatever the problem was it wasn't important enough for the other members of the group to make a serious attempt at finding her. But she made good time through the nighttime traffic, avoiding Seccie and EF troop patrols with the ease born of long practice.

There was no obvious sign of trouble when they touched down outside the Fortress. Two of the older Hex children, both girls, were standing guard by the door and they saluted as Raven exited the flitter. The movement gave her pause for thought and she stopped, regarding them.

"Apparently a meeting is going on," she said. "Do you know what it's about?"

"Finn and Jeeva, the Snake gangers, brought in a boy about an hour ago," the older of the two told her. "After that Alaric and Wraith arrived, so perhaps the meeting is to debrief a new Hex," she suggested.

Raven looked at the girl for a while. She looked about fourteen and, like Raven, she had dark hair and dark eyes.

"You're observant," she commented. "It's Cara, isn't it?"

"Yes," the girl smiled, pleased to have been recognized.

"I remember you from your training," Raven told her. "You were one of the fastest to learn. Are you as good with that gun?" She gestured at the laser pistol the girl was holding firmly.

"I'm better," Cara said, grinning. "But it's not as hard to learn weapons."

Raven raised an eyebrow.

"The net *is* a weapon," she said dryly. "It just has a different sort of trigger."

Both children looked at her with wide eyes but Raven was already turning away, heading inside. Cloud had to take a few fast paces to catch her up.

"What were you trying to teach them?" he asked when he reached her.

"To think," she replied. "Those kids may find their lives changing very soon."

"We all might," Could said under his breath as he watched her head up the stairs. Then he turned back to where the door guards kept their posts. He doubted he would be welcome at whatever meeting was being held. In the circumstances he might as well see if Raven had succeeded in encouraging thought.

The door to one of the smaller meeting rooms was open and, when Raven paused in the doorway, she saw Alaric, Wraith, Ali and a stranger. Not precisely a stranger though. As Raven stood, unobserved for the moment, her eidetic memory recalled where she had been this boy before. He was the intruder who had triggered a low-level security alert a few days ago. When Jordan had shown her the surveillance footage Raven had felt a tremble of recognition and had wondered if he might be a Hex. Now, before she had even had time to check up on him, he had appeared.

"Is this our emergency?" she asked and all four people turned around to look at her.

"Not exactly," Wraith replied, unfazed by her sudden appearance. "But Drow has brought us interesting information which I think you should hear."

Raven came into the room and swung herself up to sit on the edge of the meeting table and waited expectantly. It didn't take the others long to fill her in—Drow had described Gift and Tally's situation to them as best he understood it and then they had questioned him about his meeting with them in the net. It was that aspect that most interested Raven and her dark eyes remained fixed on the boy as he stammered his own description of the encounter.

"Interesting," she said eventually and Alaric smiled at her.

"We thought you'd think so," he said.

"We've contacted Drow's family and apparently a gang member called Rosso called in about twenty minutes ago and requested payment for helping Gift and Tally," Ali added. "It appears for the time being they're safe."

"It was well thought of," Wraith said, looking approvingly at the boy. "It was brave of you to try so hard to help them despite the danger to yourself."

"I didn't think it was all that dangerous," Drow confessed, tearing his eyes away from Raven who had held him transfixed since she had first entered the room. "I only found out I was a Hex today. But my family, they've suspected for ages and not said anything. They helped immediately when I asked them to. Tally and Gift only had me."

"And now they have us," Wraith assured him. "Don't you agree, Raven?"

"Hmm?" Raven blinked and looked at him blankly for a moment before nodding. "Yes," she said quickly. "It shouldn't prove too problematic to help them, despite the distances involved but—"

"But what?" Drow asked, alarmed, and Raven fixed him with an unreadable onyx stare.

"There's something strange about this," she mused. "If Drow met them during their first foray into the net, how did they know they were Hexes? More than that, how did they come to bear those names?"

The others glanced at each other and shrugged. Alaric was the first to speak.

"Why does it matter?" he asked.

"Because there's a mystery here," Raven replied with a flash of annoyance. "And mysteries require discovery."

"But you will help them," Drow said pleadingly and Raven smiled for the first time as his silver eyes met her black gaze.

"Yes," she said. "I promise."

The others relaxed slightly and Alaric said thoughtfully, "We had better consider how best to approach the matter. Perhaps we could combine this rescue with the trip to Transcendence."

"Which might have to happen sooner than we'd planned," Wraith agreed, rising to his feet. He glanced at Drow. "You should go with Ali," he told the boy. "She can tell you more about us and explain a little of our history. Then you'll need to repeat your story to some more of our group, if you don't mind."

"Not at all," Drow said politely, rising to follow Ali out of the room. But at the door he paused and turned back. "Raven?" he said hesitantly.

"Yes?" She turned to face him and he swallowed nervously, still obviously in awe of her.

"Do you know anything about the darkness?" he said.

"The darkness?" Raven's eyes widened and her pupils dilated slightly. Wraith, turning in surprise at the question, was alarmed to see that the color had drained out of her skin, leaving her paler than ever, like the ghost she claimed to be. "What darkness?" she whispered.

"The darkness in the net," Drow replied, looking at her with concern. "I don't know how long it's been there. But it's spreading all the time and everything it touches turns dark."

8

The Sun Became Black

Raven launched herself into the net as if
leaping from a cliff. She hadn't waited to
explain, even though Wraith and the others
had stared after her in confusion when she
ran from the room. Darkness, the word rang
in her mind like a curse. Only once before
had the net been dark to her. It had been
when Dr. Kalden, the scientist whose exper-
imentation was responsible for the death
and torture of thousands, had begun to
shred her mind. Absorbed in her own pain,
all she had been conscious of was darkness,
until she had escaped into the net and
found the strength to strike back against her
torturers.

With the preparations for the attack on
Transcendence and the media manipula-
tions required in releasing Avalon's music,

Raven had been separated from the network which was her lifeblood too much recently. Now, as her fingertips rested lightly on the keypad, her mind hurled itself out of the shielded system of the fortress and along the flow of data. Separating herself, she sent her awareness in a hundred different directions down the data pathways, each line of thought dividing itself over and over again as she quested through the net. Information flooded through her. A million different commands and requests a second were channeled past her consciousness and each one was considered, evaluated and rejected. What she was searching for was the absence of movement: a place where the chattering of the net ceased. She spread herself further and thinner. She was the web now, thousands of different strands drawing in around the object of her search. She drew the net tighter and tighter until, with a shock, she hit a wall.

The message sped through her brain, informing each tendril of the search that something unusual had been found. The different parts of Raven ceased their own progress through the dataflow and reached toward the point of contact. Gradually her mind coagulated until she was standing at the edge of the blackness. It rolled over the light and movement of the net, extinguishing everything in its path for an instant as its darkness fogged the datastreams. Raven watched its approach. It quested blindly, snail-like in its progress, but huge and inexorable. As it came nearer Raven blurred her own presence, hiding within a shield she had constructed of misleading access routines and bounced commands. Now that she was invisible to almost every presence in the network and cloaked in a blur of light she moved closer still and reached out to brush the edge of the cloud.

> **dark—death—black** < it whispered and she pulled back.

She felt numbed by even that slight contact but it wasn't enough. She needed more information. Doubling her shield, she steeled herself to enter the cloud of contagion. Then, taking a deep breath, she leapt forward and fell into the well of darkness.

It overwhelmed her. Fragments of thought echoed forward and backward inside the darkness. The only mind it had was this roiling fog of words.

> **dark down in the darkness of death ... roving searching questing . . . question? question? . . . black/attack/turned on the rack ... darkness here darkness here darkness** <

Reaching out delicately Raven inserted a single word into the fog.

HEX

> light? <

The response was like a thunderstorm,
flashing of thoughts coursing through the
darkness, giving it motion and speed with
the violence of its reactions.

> light blight spite . . . here the dark-
ness here the darkness here the darkness
here . . . flowing/moving/enfolding/dim-
ming . . . stopping the quick/light/color . . .
stilling the city that sings . . . clipping the
wings . . . darkness brings . . . <

The ominous words rolled on, forward
and backward, as the cloud continued its
passage, leaving the net dark behind it for
microseconds until the data currents recovered and flashed back into active life. Raven
could measure a perceptible time-lag
caused by the cloud. It wasn't yet long
enough to seriously interfere with the operation of the net, measurable only in the
microseconds of data transfer. But the
period was increasing. The cloud was growing and, the larger it became, the longer its
effects lasted. Raven could imagine that
this thing was capable of dimming the
entire net if its growth rate continued. But
what was it?

A horrible suspicion was growing in her
mind and she moved out of the cloud to
consider it, allowing it to creep on without
her. She stood in the wasteland it left

behind, waiting as the lights around her reappeared. Then, slowly, she circled around to the front of the darkness. Reaching for the strands of the web, she pulled them to her, filling her presence with the flow of data currents. Cloaked in light she stood before it and presented an interrogation like the point of sword.

> who/what/why are you? <

The question fell into the pit of the cloud and echoed back to her.

> why ... what ... who ... you? <

Raven reached further into the net and drew more of it toward her. A thousand minor access routines were diverted to flow about her position so that she stood in a cloud of light facing the darkness. Flourishing her sword once more she announced:

> I am Raven—I rule here—identify yourself <

With a roar the cloud engulfed her and all the lights went out. The sword she had created splintered and shattered, its fragments melting like ice into nothingness. Around her the darkness beat against her cloak and shield until they also were shredded and fell away, leaving her defenseless before a rage that was like a force of nature.

> RAVEN RAVEN RAVEN RAVEN RAVEN RAVEN RAVEN RAVEN RAVEN RAVEN RAVEN RAVEN RAVEN RAVEN

RAVEN RAVEN RAVEN RAVEN RAVEN
RAVEN   RAVEN   RAVEN   RAVEN
RAVEN . . . <

Her own name beat against her brain
over and over again. The cloud buffeted her
about with the power of its fury; throwing
images of darkness, death and pain at her
until she screamed with the sensory overload. She flew for the edge of the blackness
but, as in a storm, she was dragged back
into the whirling eye of the hurricane. It
was trying to break her and the moment she
realized that she let go.

Her fingers lifted from the keypad and
her connection to the net, a constant humming presence in the back of her mind,
locked shut. She had closed out the horror
that dwelt within the network by shutting
out everything. Now she stood, completely
alone, staring at the computer screen. Something inside the net hated her and it would
stop at nothing to destroy her. Even if that
meant destroying the net in the process.

The Minister for Internal Affairs was a
busy man. His children were at an age
where the cost of their education seemed to
double in price every year. His position had
led his friends and family to expect lavish
hospitality from him and he had married a

trophy wife who had found spending his money a major attraction. In order to avoid running even further into debt he had embezzled money from several different sectors of the government and accepted bribes from people who even the corrupt EF elite considered dubious. The continued strain on his nerves from his tangled personal affairs had led him into an expensive drug habit, which in turn had allowed him to be blackmailed.

But these were the problems that came with high office and the Minister understood that it was necessary to make sacrifices. What was annoying him right now was that he has expected to deal with another department's work as well as his own. Charles Alverstead, the governor of the CPS, had angered the President of the Federation with his continued excuses for his failure to locate the rogue Hexes. President Sanatos was not a man it was healthy to annoy. He had put the entire cabinet on notice that he expected this Hex named Raven to be found and would brook no further incompetence. So all across Europe criminals and agitators were openly criticizing the Federation and the Minister for Internal Affairs could do nothing about it while his entire staff were occupied in the quest. Every minute another ten false leads and foolish suggestions came to rest on his desk. Now a functionary was bringing in yet another.

"What is it now?" he barked. "A suggestion that we search for this Raven in London Zoo aviary? Or perhaps a report from a Seccie in Australia that he saw a girl with black hair and dark eyes two years ago but he can't remember where?"

The functionary quailed, hugging the data-pad he carried closely to his thin chest.

"Uh, no, Minister . . ." he stammered. "Not exactly. It's not really to do with this Raven character."

"Then why are you bothering me with it?" the Minister roared. "Don't you know I have a meeting with the President in—" he paused to check the ornate chronometer hanging on the wall of his office, "in ten minutes?" He slammed his fist down on his desk. "Are you perhaps not aware that I am not permitted by his Excellency to work on any subject other than the apprehension of this mutant? Well, man? What have you got to say for yourself?"

"It's the other Hexes, Sir," the functionary gasped.

"It's the other Hexes?" The Minister drew his brows together in a massive frown.

"The Freedom ones," the functionary

told him. "Possible descendants of Theo Freedom? The Minister of Propaganda passed on a list of possible candidates on his arrest list?"

"What of them?" The Minister for Internal Affairs had stopped shouting. Instead he was almost standing, leaning forward across his desk, his eyes intent on the datapad the functionary carried.

"Well, we've found two of them," the functionary said simply, presenting the pad. "It's not much of a lead, I know. But it's the only one we have so far and I thought you might want to—"

"Give me that!" The Minister snatched the pad out of his subordinate's hands and read through the data quickly. "Goddammit," he breathed. "This might actually be worth something. Get me Alverstead on the vidcom. No, wait! Get me the Head of the Security Services. Let's bring these two in for questioning first. Once they're secure we can worry about whether they're the right ones."

Wraith knocked softly on the door to Raven's room. There was no answer but he didn't allow that to stop him. When she had departed so abruptly he'd questioned Drow about the thing he'd seen in the net and the very idea of it alarmed him. Raven's reaction had been even more violent than his and the closest terminal was the one in her room. He knocked again, louder, then paused to call:

"Raven, open the door."

It had been a long time since he had tried to tell his wild sister what to do and he was doubtful if he'd get any response at all. But after a few moments he heard footsteps approaching and the door slid open. Raven was standing in the doorway but from her expression Wraith could tell her mind was miles away. She looked like a statue, staring through him at some unimaginable distance.

"What is it?" he asked quietly and her eyes tracked to meet his.

"Death," she said softly. "Death and darkness, that's all it knows."

"Is it dangerous?"

"More than you can possibly imagine." A bitter smile suddenly appeared on Raven's face and she laughed mockingly. The laughter seemed to pull her out of whatever trance she'd been in and she looked at him directly as she said, "We've talked about shutting down the net in the past to combat the EF. What would happen if we tried and succeeded?"

"Communications would be disrupted?"

Wraith replied. "A lot of information would be lost." He frowned. "What are you getting at?"

"The end of the world," she told him. "If the net goes dark that's a catastrophe. It's not just that the speed of information retrieval is slowed, or that some data is lost, it's everything. Economies are solely electronic—it's the net that keeps track of creds, without the net we lose that. Food as well, all production and distribution is controlled by the network, without it we have stacks of food rotting on one side of the country and famine on the other. What else?" She shook her head at the enormity of it. "All public services shut down, all vidcoms, all terminals, every media outlet in the world. Even those areas that the EF doesn't control use the same net. Without it, there's chaos."

"And you think that might be about to happen?" Wraith took Raven's shoulders and pulled her around so that he could look straight into those obsidian eyes. "This darkness is going to engineer a net crash?"

"If it can," she confirmed. "If it hates enough." The twisted smile reappeared and her eyes glazed over. "And it does," she whispered.

"How can it hate?" Wraith asked in confusion. "What does it hate? Raven, what *is* it?"

The Hex held herself perfectly still as she answered, the words painfully dragged out of her in an admission which she would have given almost anything not to make.

"It's Kalden," she said. "What's left of him. He's back. And how can you kill someone who's already dead?"

Gift sometimes wondered if Tally had always been like this. Had there ever been a time, when they were babies maybe, when her automatic response to everything hadn't been to worry? Sometimes he doubted it. As long as he could remember he had been traveling with Tally's anxiety. Sometimes it seemed as if it had more of a personality than she did. Now, when everything was going well at last, when they were safe and about to strike back against the Federation for the first time in their lives, she was still incapable of doing anything but fretting.

With a sigh he threw down his cards and took Tally's out of her hand. She blinked and looked at him in surprise.

"Have we finished?" she asked.

"No," he told her. "We haven't finished. But it's actually impossible to play a game with a person who stares into space all the time and keeps biting her nails and picking at the mattress. What's the matter with you?"

"I'm sorry," Tally sighed. "I don't mean to be annoying, really I don't. But I keep thinking of what's going to happen next and . . ." she shrugged, "here we're just waiting, we have no way of contacting anyone and no idea what's going on." Suddenly she stood up. "I think we should find a public vidcom and call Drow," she said.

"For God's sake, Tally!" Gift exclaimed, slamming his fist on the floor in anger. "Haven't we discussed this already? Didn't we agree that we weren't safe on the streets where any Seccie patrol could pick us up? Would you please at least wait until it's daylight and we can hide in the crowds. Or maybe try to get some sleep?" His tone became sarcastic. "That's a radical suggestion, I know, but it's past midnight in London as well as here. Drow will be asleep just as you should be. One thing's for certain. He's not insisting that someone stays up and plays a card game with him which he can't even be bothered to concentrate on for more than half a damned second!"

"He's also not carrying the most important piece of data any Hex could imagine," Tally hissed in a fierce whisper. "And I don't care how nasty you get, Gift. Something's not right here, I'm certain of it. Every second that passes just makes me more and more certain that somewhere something's gone wrong." She whirled around and began packing their few possessions into the pack, glaring at him through her tangle of auburn hair. "I'm going to make a call to Drow," she told him. "And you can't stop me."

Gift closed his eyes and counted to ten silently. She was right that he couldn't stop her. It was obviously futile to argue. He could try to overpower her but he didn't like the idea of using force on his own sister and Tally was strong enough to escape him unless he tied her down or knocked her out. In the circumstances he only had one option and, crossing to sit beside her, he began to help her pack.

"Listen to me carefully," he said as he did so. "Whether you're right or wrong, I'm getting tired of this emotional blackmail. I'm warning you, Tally, this constant worrying of yours is making you hell to be with. If you could stop fearing ghosts and shadows for a while you'd be a lot less insane."

"Maybe I am insane," Tally said quietly, buckling the worn straps of the pack. "But when the EF's after you it doesn't hurt to be paranoid."

The warehouse was dark as they made their way down the rusty staircase and toward the massive double doors. Gift unbarred them and pushed them open enough for them both to slip through, then pushed them closed behind him. Hefting their pack on his shoulders he began to retrace a route back into the center of town, where he had seen vidcoms. Tally followed close behind him but she didn't try to initiate a conversation. Just as well, he thought, or I might have to strangle her. He trudged along grimly, thinking angry thoughts about sisters who made you wander around town in the middle of the night because they had funny feelings. But as they approached the town center something caught his attention and he stopped walking. Immediately Tally walked into him from behind and gasped.

"Shhh," he warned her. "Look at that."

The sky was unusually bright, as if from the glare of many streetlights and, ahead of them, he could hear indistinct voices.

"Something's going on," Tally said, stating the obvious, and Gift rolled his eyes.

"No kidding," he replied. "Keep quiet and let's go find out what."

Walking on a little further they came to the edge of a small square and Gift looked cautiously around the edge of a building. Immediately he pulled back and turned to look at Tally with wide surprised eyes.

"There are three Seccie skimmers

around that corner," he told her. "And about nine Seccies just standing about."

"Can you hear what they're saying?" Tally whispered and Gift shrugged.

"I'll try," he told her. "Keep well out of sight and I'll try to get closer."

Tally tried to grab his arm and stop him but Gift was already away, moving under the cover of shadow around the side of the building. Clutching their pack and shrinking into the corner she waited for him. After about ten minutes he returned, slipping silently around the corner like a shadow.

"Not good news," he said softly. "Come on, follow me." He turned away from the square and Tally hastened after him as he worked his way through the narrower streets until they were well out of earshot. Only then did he tell her what he had overheard. "A whole load of EF troops have arrived in town and the Seccies have been told to keep out of the way. The troops are closing down the borders in a hunt for some dangerous criminals." He looked grim. "I think we can probably guess who they mean."

"How did they find us?" Tally asked, horrified.

"Ask your paranoia," Gift replied. "I have no idea. But we'd better get out of this rat trap as quickly as we can."

"We can go cross-country to Verona," Tally suggested. "It'll take a long time but we'll do better to keep off the roads."

"We'll have to get past the troops here first," Gift reminded her. "But at least we've had warning. Your funny feelings might just have saved our lives."

Drow was still getting over the shock of realizing how many Hexes there were and how organized the group was. He'd had a vague idea that the Ghosts were a large gang—they controlled too much territory to be anything else—but the sheer amount of people and technology they possessed staggered the imagination. Ali, the blonde girl in white who had interested him what seemed like years ago, had tried to explain the organization to him but before she had finished a mass meeting had been called and he'd been unable to retain much of the information.

Now, seated at the front of a large meeting hall filled with people, he tried to work out what was going on. It was clear that the Ghosts were divided into two main factions. One of the terrorists, Anglecynn they called themselves, who were mostly adults without Hex abilities but with impressive weaponry and the skills to use them. The other faction was the Hexes themselves: kids for the most part and the people who seemed to be the leaders of the group. Those leaders confused him the most. Alaric and Geraint, the Anglecynn leaders, were like every gang-boss he'd encountered; taking their strength from the confidence of their followers. But the leaders of the Hex faction seemed to be considered with an almost mystical awe by the younger Hexes. He supposed that made sense if every last one of those children owed their lives to the skill of the people now standing on the platform in front of him, but he found the group strange. There was Wraith: a ganger in appearance but he seemed as honest as a priest. Ali and Luciel were corpkids, the kind of people he'd have thought couldn't last five minutes on the streets, but they talked like generals in a war; and Kez, a streetrat, who seemed completely at ease with them. Then there was Avalon, the rock star, who was in some way the inspiration of the group, and Cloud, her friend, who appeared to have almost no role whatsoever. Finally there was Raven.

Drow still didn't know what he thought about Raven. The group seemed unable to move without her. Every word she spoke was treated as some kind of sacred pronouncement and Ali's description of the

Ghosts had been punctuated with constant repetitions of "Raven says." But they all did that. On the platform Wraith was saying it now.

"Raven believes that the danger in the net is unlikely to become a serious problem before the mission to Transcendence and that controlling the orbital satellite network might well give us a better idea of how to combat the menace. Therefore we've decided to go ahead. The longer we delay the more danger there is that the EF will locate us. According to Raven the search for us has been stepped up across Europe . . ."

Drow tuned out again. He was frankly amazed that a group of Hexes this large had been able to survive for as long as they had. Whatever this mission to Transcendence was, he hoped for their sake it would succeed. His own concern was for Gift and Tally and it was that which had convinced Wraith to allow him to go with them.

"You're very inexperienced," he had said with regret. "But Raven says you must be a strong Hex to have achieved as much as you have and, of all of us, you're the only one to have had contact with Gift and Talent. They trust you and they don't know us. As for the real purpose of the mission, we'll have to explain that on the way. We're out of time now."

The clock was certainly ticking. Ali had whispered to him as they entered the meeting that this was more to prepare for the results of their mission than to discuss its wisdom. Apparently Raven had said or done something which meant that the journey to Transcendence was certain to happen and, through hacking the net, the group had obtained seats on a plane which would leave that very evening.

Drow blinked as he realized that Wraith had finished speaking and that Raven had taken his place at the front of the platform. One thing he agreed with the Ghost on was that Raven was everything he had imagined a Hex to be. She looked competent and dangerous and there was something about her that didn't seem entirely sane. She stood in silence until the murmurs of the crowd had died down, then began to speak in a very different manner from the others.

"To most of you here the name of Doctor Kalden doesn't mean much. The stuff of nightmares perhaps but a danger that no longer concerns us. But apparently when I killed him I didn't do it thoroughly enough. He died in the course of conducting a dangerous experiment, the results of which were unpredictable and intended to satisfy torturers and politicians rather than scientific enquiry. The subject of this experiment . . ." Raven blinked for a second, a hesitation that would be almost imperceptible to anyone unfamiliar with her normal measured speech, then continued. "The subject was linked to a machine intended to affect and control the bioelectrical energies of the mind. But the subject took control of the machine and created a link to the net, something unanticipated. At the moment of his death, some fragments of his consciousness took advantage of that connection and were preserved inside the net.

"There's not much of him left now, barely even what could be called a consciousness. Yet, in a way, it is conscious, although all it knows is hate. The reason I'm telling you this is that from now on the net isn't safe for any of us. Kalden's mind is now the focus of a dark cloud, eating its way through the network. So far the damage it has caused is barely noticeable but that will change. No group, agency or government exists that can stop it. But we can. Once we hold the orbital satellite network we will move to eradicate it. But for now, stay clear of the darkness."

Jordan had stayed on duty throughout the meeting. It was procedure that a small team monitor communications and news nets at all time. In the past that had proved important. But this time Jordan wondered if they'd have been better off not knowing this piece of news. The Ghosts had come out of the meeting in a positive mood. Most of them seemed confident that Raven's team would succeed at taking control of the net and wiping out this new menace with no difficulty whatsoever. This latest news was bound to bring down that mood.

But Jordan had no choice. As the Ghosts streamed out of the meeting she made her way inside to where the mission team were clustered around the platform. Alaric looked up and smiled as she arrived, then his face clouded over.

"Looks like you have bad news," he said.

"I do," Jordan replied reluctantly, looking at Drow. "News came in from some underground contacts in Europe that the EF have congregated some forces in an unlikely area." She swallowed and then added, not looking at any of them, "They've sent a troop detachment to the city of Padua. It looks as if Tally and Gift have been found."

9

I Stand at the Door

In the year 2300, to commemorate the founding of the European Federation, the government had decided to build a European city that would stand as an example of their wealth and might. Transcendence, the culmination of that dream, had been created in the south of France. Seventy years later it had swelled to become the largest of the European megaplexes and, in actuality, the largest city in the world. Like an iceberg, much of its colossal size was underground. But the inhabitants didn't care about being cut off from the sun. Transcendence was dedicated to technology. No windows allowed the crude light of day to penetrate where artificial lighting could be endlessly adjusted to the precise requirements of the citizens. Equally, the grassy slopes of the

French countryside didn't interest a population who increasingly sought the pleasures of virtual realities created for them in holoparks underneath the ground.

It was a playground for the rich. Only the most successful companies were allowed to own business space there, only individuals with an impeccable security record were permitted to work there and throughout the city the Seccies kept watch with a diligence not seen in any other megaplex. No inch of Transcendence was left unwatched or unguarded—hidden in the walls of the arcology were surveillance devices constantly monitoring the well-being of their citizens. The government of the EF boasted that no crime ever committed in Transcendence had been unpunished for more than twenty-four hours.

It was to this city, owned and controlled by the EF like a willing slave, that Raven and her companions came. For Wraith their arrival brought back old memories of the time he and Raven had first come to London. Sitting next to Raven as the stratojet began its descent, he touched her arm lightly.

"It's as if we're beginning again," he said under his breath, and she glanced sideways at him.

"Or finishing what we started," she

replied and turned to look over her shoulder, at the seats behind them. Alaric and Jordan sat together, dressed like an affluent young professional couple. Neither of them had extensive Seccie files and the fake IDs Raven had constructed for them should be enough to fool even the most thorough of investigations. Wraith was glad they were there. They were both skilled with several different kinds of weaponry and their experience as terrorists made them versatile companions for this kind of mission. Behind them sat Luciel and Kez. It had been harder to construct believable fake identities for them since their youth made them unlikely corporates. It had been Ali who'd come up with the ideal disguise. Among its many celebrated institutions Transcendence contained one of the most renowned European universities: the Academy of Progressive Thought. It had been the work of moments for Raven to enter the boys' identities on the academic roll. They were dressed as young students whose wealthy families had been able to afford the exorbitant fees the university charged and the IDs claimed that they were physics students, a masquerade which their recent devotion to education would enable them to perform creditably. Wraith smiled to himself as he watched them, thinking how much they had changed.

Luciel, idly watching the stratojet's in-flight entertainment screens, was a very different person from the tortured experimental subject they had rescued, addicted against his will to dangerous and life-threatening drugs. Kez, beside him, his bronze hair shining in the low lights of the jet, had changed the most. No one would recognize in this sober and self-assured young student the streetrat whom Raven had picked up on a whim.

Wraith looked further back and his smile faded. Drow sat on his own, behind Luciel and Kez, staring blankly into space. Back in London Jordan was monitoring the call-code they had given Gift and Tally, hoping against hope that they had escaped the siege in Padua. It was for that reason that Drow had been included on the mission, although Wraith doubted if there was much chance of rescuing the two young Hexes about whom he knew little more than their names. Drow had similar doubts and Wraith recognized the mixture of guilt and shame that the boy had displayed when he heard about the EF's action to surround Padua. He had felt the same way himself when he had failed to return Rachel, his youngest sister, to sanity after Kalden's experiments. Drow seemed barely conscious of their presence. He had not even objected to having his long black hair cut short and the silver circuitry removed from his braids in the interests of concealing his identity. His fake ID had been the most difficult of all to invent. Finally, Raven had fallen back on an old ruse and identified Drow as a hopeful young actor, journeying to Transcendence to play a minor role in one of the vids produced there by a successful media company.

Wraith sighed ruefully and looked at himself in the reflective window of the stratojet. He also had submitted to having his hair cut, shaved so close to his head that its unusual white color was barely noticeable. But, if Drow's identity had been the hardest to construct, his and Raven's were the most dangerous. They both wore the black uniforms of EF soldiers, their rank tags identifying them as Force Commanders in the Intelligence Division. Raven had risked the impersonation because it had seemed the safest way to avoid any detailed checks into their background. Intelligence Officers were feared even by Seccies for their ability to interrogate anyone under any circumstances and the fact they were answerable only to their own superiors and the EF President.

A dull roaring noise came from the engines of the jet and Wraith glanced at Raven.

"Landing in five minutes," she told him. Her fingertips rested on the vidscreen on the stand in front of her seat. To any observer she would have appeared to be adjusting the controls of the entertainment unit but in fact both she and Luciel were linked into the stratojet's computer systems, keeping track of its movements and its connection to the network of Transcendence itself. Throughout the mission the Hexes would endeavor to keep in constant touch with the network. If their impersonations were discovered it might give them enough warning to escape with their lives.

"Anything unusual?" Wraith asked and Raven shook her head.

"No, but several things we should be aware of," she replied. "For instance, security has recently been increased in all important EF installations and cities in order to combat the threat from the rogue Hex, Raven."

"I see," Wraith smiled wryly. "How do the activities of this dangerous criminal affect us in particular?"

"A Seccie squad is stationed on permanent duty at the arrivals terminal," Raven informed him. "As senior officers they may offer us escort."

"How should we refuse it?" Wraith asked, lowering his voice.

"Refuse it?" Raven arched an eyebrow at him quizzically. "We are senior Intelligence Officers, our intention is to tour the Space Operations Center to assess its vulnerability to terrorist attack. How better to do so than with a Seccie squad in attendance?"

Ali rubbed her eyes, trying to make sense of the data-pad in front of her. But the information kept blurring out of focus. Irritably she threw it down on the table in front of her and was startled as a soft voice commented dryly:

"There's nothing wrong with the screen, you're just too tired to make sense of it. Why don't you try and get some rest?"

"Perhaps because I'm trying to do five people's jobs at once?" Ali replied. "And prepare for God knows what if Raven's team fails."

"It must be difficult to prepare for an unpredictable situation," Cloud said sympathetically.

"Yes, it—" Ali broke off and then smiled ruefully. "It's impossible, isn't it?"

"I think your time could be put to better use," Cloud admitted. "Such as getting some rest maybe?"

"I've only been awake for five hours,"

Ali pointed out. "I don't need rest."

"You've been working solidly for all that time," Cloud reminded her. "At least go and find something to eat and take your brain off the hook for a while." He glanced around the control room. "Is anything drastically important likely to occur in the next hour?"

"No," Ali admitted.

"Would your assistants be capable of summoning you if it did?" he continued, gesturing at Avalon and the three Hex children who were manning the control room.

"Yes."

"In that case, go and rest. Watch the vid or something," he told her. "Unless you're worried I'll take advantage of your absence to call the Seccies and tell them where you are?"

Ali blinked at him in surprise and he laughed out loud.

"That was a joke," he added.

"I know," Ali replied and sighed. "OK, you win, I'll go and rest—"

"If anything happens we'll call you," Cloud replied.

Stretching, Ali climbed out of the chair she'd been sitting in. She felt as if her muscles had been turned to jelly. All morning she'd been reading reports and contingency plans until they had stopped making any sense. Cloud was probably right, she admitted to herself, she did need to rest. Wandering into the living area of the Fortress, she dialed a cup of coffee from the Nutromac and slumped in one of the large armchairs. The moment control to the vidscreen was lying beside her and she considered it for a while. Recently she hadn't felt like watching any of the channels. The media was locked down by EF law and she was getting tired of watching news that never criticized the government or reported the activities of those who did. However, one of the entertainment channels might be amusing for a while, she thought. Touching the control, she keyed the vidscreen on.

The logo of Populix appeared on the screen and Ali hesitated. She hadn't meant to watch the channel her father owned or to watch the news at all. But whoever had last been using the screen had obviously left it at that setting and Ali left it there as she tried to decide what to watch. In a few seconds her decision had been made for her. Instead of the familiar face of one of the announcers the screen displayed a single line of text:

This channel has ceased transmissions by order of the Security Services for broadcasts not in accordance with EF regulations.

Ali stared at it for a while, her mind at

first unable to assimilate the meaning of the words. Then finally she slumped back in the chair. The control fell from her hands and she didn't bother to pick it up or change the channel. She heard the hiss of the door slide open behind her but her eyes didn't leave the screen.

"Ali," Avalon's voice asked. "What's happened?"

"Populix has been shut down," Ali replied, turning to face her. "Probably because of their broadcasts of your songs."

Avalon's eyes dropped and she said quietly, "I'm sorry."

"No, don't be." Ali stood up and forced a half-smile. "You didn't do anything wrong."

"Isn't Populix one of the channels your father owns?" Avalon asked. "Could this affect him?"

"Maybe." Ali shrugged awkwardly. "I don't know."

"Do you want us to find out?" Avalon asked. "There'll be news somewhere on the network."

"No, Raven said we shouldn't use the net," Ali replied. "Besides, I'm not sure I want to know." She was silent for a moment and then she continued. "When the CPS took me away I was angry at my father for not trying to stop them. But recently, when we rescued Charis—and now that he might be in danger himself—I don't think about it the same way. There really wasn't anything he *could* do. That's what it means to live in a tyranny." She laughed suddenly. "Isn't that strange? I've been working against the government for four years now but it's only recently that I realized we were right."

"That's what Wraith believes," Avalon replied. "We just tend to forget it when we're fighting to save our own lives. Maybe we should remember we're fighting for right more often."

"Except Raven," Ali said without bitterness, as a statement of fact. "She's fighting for herself."

"I suppose that makes sense," Avalon replied. "Raven's unique after all. If she doesn't support her own cause who will?"

"We will," Ali replied. "That's the point. Even when it's useless. A tyranny only succeeds when people stay silent while injustice goes on, the way my father stayed silent when I was taken for extermination. But yesterday Populix made the opposite decision. They tried to fight and they've been crushed." She looked back at the screen. "But at least they tried," she said softly.

"And so will we," Avalon replied.

"Yeah." Ali hunched her shoulders resolutely. "Come on," she said. "Let's get back to work. Somehow I don't feel like resting right now."

Tally and Gift made their way through the street quickly, checking constantly to see if they were being watched. When a tourist so much as glanced in their direction they hurried away, keeping their heads down and trying to make themselves look as small as possible. The trek to Verona had not been pleasant. On the edge of Padua they had reached the transport terminus just in time to see the last lev-train preparing to depart. EF troops were closing down the facility but were having difficulty finding staff to shut down all the machinery. The lev-trains were automated and stopped only briefly at the station before whizzing off into the night. Softly as shadows, Tally and Gift had climbed up into one of the freight-cars and hid, expecting to be discovered any minute. But the terminus manager with the key to shut down the trains had been late and as he arrived, panting and wheezing, the elevated train finished its automatic unloading and sped off with the twins on board.

The lev-train continued on through the night, humming quietly and almost soothing the children to sleep. But sometime before dawn they worked out that the train would turn soon and head north through the mountains to Switzerland without passing through another Italian city. That could last for days and Tally knew that with every moment that passed the chances of their discovery increased. So the twins waited for a smooth stretch of countryside and jumped from the train, turning in the direction of Verona.

They had stumbled on throughout the night, keeping off the roads, worried all the time that they would hear the EF troops behind them. Gift had ditched the pack with their possessions in to make better speed and, half dead with fatigue, they had staggered on. Now all they carried was a few creds, the precious data disk and the scrap of paper with Drow's call-code.

"Look, Tally," Gift said in a whisper, despite the bustling crowds around them. "Vidcom booths."

Tally looked up wearily and saw the row of shiny booths ahead of them.

"Thank God," she said. "At last."

They had to wait for one of the booths to be empty and they leaned against the outside of one of them, trying to stay upright. The first one to be vacated had been being used by a large Italian woman and as she squeezed herself out of the booths she looked at them with disgust. Tally quailed beneath her disdainful stare but Gift looked the woman back straight in the eye and she stalked off with a huff. He knew they weren't much to look at, dirty and bedraggled as they were, but he wasn't ashamed to be stared at. He was too relieved to be alive to care what a stranger thought of his appearance.

The twins crowded into the small booth and Tally dragged out the scrap of paper while Gift punched in the code.

> Eu/Lon-node/Bethnel/chr#4856 <

It seemed to take an age to connect but when it finally did it wasn't Drow who looked back at them. Although they didn't know what their friend looked like he couldn't be the person who was staring back at them from the vidcom screen. This was a girl: her ash-blonde hair brushed back neatly from her face but dark shadows under her eyes making her look almost as tired as they were.

"Gift and Talent?" she said when she saw them and abruptly her face broke into a smile. "Thank God, we were hoping you would call. Are you all right?"

"Just about," Gift replied suspiciously. "But who are you?"

"I'm Ali," the girl said. "Drow contacted my people and they went to look for you but we were afraid you'd been captured."

"Your people?" Tally asked eagerly. "Are you the Hexes we were looking for?"

"Yes," the girl said. "I think so, at least. We've been working against the Federation for some time but there isn't time to explain that to you now. This is a safe signal but you must be in danger. Where are you?"

"In Verona," Gift explained. "We had to leave Padua quickly. Someone must have recognized us."

Ali frowned, considering.

"Our team is in Transcendence right now," she said. "Is there a safe place near you where you can wait for them to get to you?"

"I think we've had enough of safe places," Gift replied.

"We'd rather keep moving," Tally agreed. "But . . ." She glanced down at herself and made a face.

"Yeah," Gift said. "We look pretty scruffy and we can't afford to buy anything better."

"All right," Ali said thoughtfully. "Does the vidcom you're using have a credstick slot?"

"Yes, it does," Gift told her. "But we don't have a credstick."

"Do you have enough money to buy one?"

"I think so," Tally said, checking through their meager funds. "Yes, we do."

"In that case go and get one and call me again when you've succeeded," Ali told them. "I'll book you tickets on the next flight out of there and wire you enough creds to get better clothes." She smiled reassuringly. "We'll get you out of there, I promise."

Avalon was relieved when Ali relayed the news that the kids were safe, at least for the time being. But when she saw the young Hex preparing to enter the net she became anxious.

"You said yourself Raven had forbidden it," she warned. "That thing is still in there somewhere."

"Raven didn't *forbid* it, she advised against it," Ali pointed out. "And she went into the net herself to create new IDs for the team. Besides," she shrugged, "what choice have I got?"

"There must be other ways to help the twins," Avalon said but Ali shook her head.

"They want to leave Verona as soon as possible and they won't be safe until they meet up with Raven's team," Ali replied. "That means booking them on to a fast jet out and without IDs they can't do that themselves. But through the net I can hack

into the transport system and arrange tickets which they can pick up at the airport."
She looked around the room. "Does anyone
have a better idea?"

Cloud raised his eyebrows but didn't
say anything and the three Hex children on
duty murmured their apologies.

"In that case, I'm going in," Ali told
them and deliberately reached out to the
terminal in front of her.

It was never as easy for Ali to achieve
the almost psychic bond Raven had with
computers. The dark-haired Hex could
interface with the net in an instant. But it
took Ali a few minutes of sustained medita-
tion before she could feel the network opening itself to her and it was difficult for her to
see the metaphor of the city of light the
other Hexes described. Slowly she felt her
way into the net and reached out toward
Italy. Ali wasn't much of a hacker but Raven
had taught them that a Hex didn't need to
be. Manipulating the net from inside was
very different from the way a normal
hacker attempted to influence strange computer systems. Ali's progress toward the
systems that controlled European transportation was slow and ponderous but she
got there eventually and slid past the security protocols easily. Once she was in the
system it was the work of moments to can-

cel the bookings for two people leaving on the next stratojet for Transcendence and substitute fake names with Gift and Talent's descriptions.

She didn't have Raven's experience in creating fake IDs but it was easier to invent false identities for children than for adults. She informed the transportation system computer that the twins were Edward and Elsie Anderson, traveling from the residence of one of their parents to that of the other. Then, backing out of the transportation system node, she inserted fake identities for their parents into the network's public access database. One parent she made an art dealer in Verona and the other a corporate businessman working in Transcendence. Deciding that was sufficient to keep Gift and Talent safe, she stopped there and headed in the direction of the Transcendence network to inform Raven that the twins had been found.

Sergeant Dwayne Crispian of the Security Services was not having a good day. He'd been on active duty for the past month and there seemed no prospect of getting leave any time soon. Just like every other Seccie team across Europe his squad was occupied in checking the IDs of every civilian they encountered in case one of them turned out to be fake. It was tedious, time-consuming work and the monotony was beginning to get to him. Therefore, when a routine check of the passenger list of the stratojet currently arriving at terminal 35 of Transcendence's airport revealed that two senior Intelligence Officers were flying in, he ordered his squad to meet them.

"That type always appreciates a little deference," he told his men. "And if we offer our services as an escort we'll at least get a break from this drone work."

Accordingly, Crispian's squad were standing at attention when the two officers arrived in the terminal. The Sergeant recognized them at once even if he hadn't been in uniform, the tall man with close cropped white hair had an authority that would have identified him, and his female companion had that look of casual menace that seemed to characterize the Intelligence Division of the EF standing army. Snapping a brisk salute Sergeant Crispian stepped forward to greet them.

"Good afternoon, Sir, Madam," he said politely. "Sergeant Crispian, Security Services, reporting. I hope you had a pleasant flight."

"As much as can be expected," the white-haired officer replied, returning his salute. "I'm Force Commander Rhys Barrow and this is Force Commander Rachel Wing."

The dark-haired woman in the black greatcoat nodded briefly to Sergeant Crispian and he swallowed nervously, meeting that black-eyed stare. She looked young for her rank but he found himself not doubting her competence. She held herself with a casual arrogance that spoke highly of her abilities and Crispian didn't like to speculate on what had earned her her position. Intelligence Officers were involved in the least pleasant of Federation work and many of them had a reputation for cruelty and sadism in carrying out their main work in extracting information from captured dissidents.

"Pleased to meet you, officers," he continued. "If I or my squad can assist you in any way I place us entirely at your disposal."

"Thank you, Sergeant," Commander Wing said curtly. "Your willingness is most appreciated." There was an ironic edge to her voice which made Crispian wonder if she was aware of his ulterior motives in offering his services but she continued smoothly: "Commander Barrow and I require an escort to the Space Operations Center. Can you have another team relieve you of your duties here?"

"Certainly, Madam," Crispian replied with another salute. "Although, there's no real need. My squad was simply checking the IDs of the passengers arriving here. Routine work since all of them will have been thoroughly vetted before being able to purchase passage to Transcendence. We can accompany you now, if you'd like."

"Shouldn't you wait for your relief?" Commander Barrow asked but his companion shook her head.

"I prefer not to wait," she told him. "If the Sergeant's duties are as routine as he describes them it won't matter if this one group of passengers isn't rechecked. None of them appear to be dangerous terrorists."

Commander Barrow laughed and Sergeant Crispian joined in quickly. Behind him his men allowed themselves discreet smiles. The Force Commander was right, Crispian thought as he fell into step behind the two officers. At a glance he could tell that this group of passengers was perfectly innocuous. Two young students had followed the Intelligence Officers off the stratojet and were chatting eagerly about their university course. He had better things to do with his time than interrogate boys about their vacation. Assisting these officers would be real work, even if they were somewhat alarming.

"Do you have any luggage, Sirs?" he asked. "We can collect it for you if you wish."

"That won't be necessary, Sergeant," Commander Barrow informed him. "This is a brief visit. We only need this." He tapped the portable terminal case he carried as if assuring himself it was still there and the Sergeant nodded.

"In that case, Commander, I'll arrange immediate transportation," he said. "We have a staff flitter on permanent duty here. I'll have it summoned immediately."

Luciel and Kez marched briskly out of the terminal. Raven and Wraith seemed not only to have gained themselves an impressive escort but managed to prevent the rest of the team from undergoing ID checks. Kez had found it hard to keep from grinning as he overheard the Seccie Sergeant's words to Raven but Luciel's constant flow of chatter about their totally fictitious career as students gave him a good excuse for his amusement.

As they left the terminal they could see Raven and Wraith ahead of them climbing into a sleek black military flitter that would presumably take them to the Space Operations Center. Luciel and Kez would be making their own way there under the guise of tourists visiting the center's museum. The plan called for Alaric and Jordan to collect a hired skimmer at the airport and for them to take a public flitter from the taxi rank. Behind them Drow would take a similar route, hopefully resulting in them all arriving at roughly the same time.

"Things seem to be going well," Luciel remarked quietly and Kez nodded.

"Things look chill for R and W," Kez replied. It had been discussed earlier that no one would use the word "Raven" while they were in Transcendence. It was possible that the surveillance devices had been calibrated to automatically alert any use of that name.

"Most impressive," Luciel agreed. "A very smooth . . ." his voice abruptly trailed off and both boys came to a halt. They had left the environs of the airport and suddenly Transcendence lay before them and they both caught their breath at the sight.

When Kez had thought of the city he had imagined it as either a larger version of London's starscrapers or as a maze of corridors that felt like being constantly indoors. The reality was very different. The space that stretched out before them was a work of art. As far as the eye could see lay a succession of spiraling staircases and gently curving walkways, each one ornamented with animated sculptures and lit with shifting patters of subtly shaded light. Even the skimmer routes and grav-tubes that hummed through the huge fretwork of carefully constructed beauty were designed with an eye to their aesthetic appeal. The boys gazed at it speechlessly, their eyes trying to make sense of the loops and swirls of architecture through which the crowds and people and vehicles rushed.

"It's amazing," Luciel breathed and Kez nodded slowly.

"Like a dream or something," he agreed.

"Incredible that the EF could have produced anything this beautiful," Luciel added and the thought brought back the recollection of their mission.

"We'd better get going," Kez said, reluctantly tearing his eyes away from the fantasy before them. "Maybe when all this is over we can look at it properly."

"Maybe," Luciel echoed but neither of them really believed it. Transcendence was stunning but it didn't seem quite real. There was too much EF power here for them to be entirely comfortable with the city's vision of mingled science and beauty. They had seen into the heart of the darkness that Transcendence's glory attempted to conceal and to them the city was a façade hiding the ugly truth of the Federation's might.

10

The Time Is at Hand

Raven leaned back into the capacious seat
of the military flitter. The chauffeur drove
carefully, as befitting someone conducting
VIPs to their destination. On either side of
the aerial vehicle a Seccie flitter kept pace
with them. Raven smiled to herself as she
opened the black case containing the
portable terminal and allowed her hands to
rest on the keypad.

So far everything was going well. Cruising gently into the Transcendence central
node, Raven could see that the local Seccies
were completely unaware that anything
was wrong. Allowing her perceptions to
link with the Transcendence surveillance
network, Raven located the other members
of their group with ease. Luciel and Kez
were sitting in a public flitter not far behind

her own, chatting innocuously about science. Alaric and Jordan had collected the rented skimmer she had arranged for them and were piloting it in accordance with all the speed regulations in the direction of the Space Center. Drow was still waiting at the airport for the public flitter but there was enough leeway in their plan to compensate for his delay. None of their conversations had been flagged as subversive by the Transcendence security system and none of their fake IDs had triggered any alerts. Satisfied, Raven began one last circuit of the local network before returning to her body and paused as something nudged the edge of her perceptions.

She frowned, unable to place the feeling she had experienced, and concentrated. Something about the data currents had struck her as familiar as she passed it. Curiously she returned, retracing her path through the net, and scanned the area. Whatever it was had disappeared. But her instincts had been roused and she began a more methodical search. Her consciousness spread outward through the net until with a start she ran into a pattern that was more familiar.

> Ali < she exclaimed. > why are you here/in the net/transcendence <

> urgent/ important/essential work <

Ali explained. > **relieved/grateful you found me—I have news** <

> ? < Raven asked wordlessly.

> **Gift/Talent found!!!** < Ali informed her joyfully. > **location Verona—I have arranged transport to you/Transcendence/city—will arrive 1800—?can you meet them?** <

> **believe/hope/think so** < Raven replied. > **inform/advise/communicate with Gift/Talent that Drow (insert picture) Hex will meet them—return now** <

She detached herself from Ali as the other Hex sped down the data current back toward England but, without Ali's knowledge, followed her pathway. Ali had obviously negotiated the net safely but Raven wasn't certain if her student was capable of evading the remains of Kalden's mind, should she encounter it. She watched from a distance as Ali returned to the Ghost computer system and vanished inside its security. Then she turned to leave.

A black tendril snaked past her. Raven pulled herself hurriedly out of its way. It moved like a snake, questing sinuously through the net, darkening for a microsecond everything it touched. The darkness was obviously spreading itself thinner. Raven wondered if Kalden had enough mind left to realize that this strategy would

be more efficient in finding her. She wasn't
sure if he was consciously looking or even
aware of the effect his twisted mind was
having on the network. But, regardless of
his intentions, this dispersal of the dark
cloud was unwelcome news. Carefully staying out of its way she moved back into the
dataflow and allowed it to carry her toward
Transcendence.

Drow leaned against the softly glowing
balustrade, his eyes blind to the appeal of
the city. His mind was full of Gift and Tally.
He feared that it was his advice that had led
them into danger and he dreaded to think
what would become of them in EF hands.
One of the first things he had asked Ali
about in London was the images of mutilated children that Populix had broadcast to
accompany the Hexes' music. Now he wished
he hadn't. Ali had turned pale as she
recounted the story of her short stay in the
experimental lab and explained a little of
what had occurred there. It was easy to
believe that the man whose mind had become
the blackness he had encountered in the network was evil. The cloud of contagion had
been terrifying enough to be a demon. The
thought that such a person had actually been
permitted to conduct experiments on chil-

dren was appalling. Now he feared that Gift and Tally had fallen victim to a similar fate.

He clenched his fists, trying not to think about it, trying not to think about anything, and then started as a voice said his name. He looked about wildly but there was no one near him. He frowned in confusion, then suddenly remembered the small transceiver that the Hexes had surgically implanted in his ear. Subvocalizing, barely moving his lips, he replied:

"Hello?"

"*At last,*" an acerbic voice remarked. "*Were you deliberately ignoring me or just wool-gathering?*"

"I—" Drow began uncomfortably but Raven's voice cut him off.

"*Forget it,*" she said. "*I have information for you. The situation has changed.*"

"Changed how?" Drow murmured. "Is something wrong?"

"*Precisely the opposite,*" Raven replied. "*Gift and Talent have been located, free and unharmed.*"

Drow was unable to prevent a gasp of relief from escaping his lips and he began to grin.

"*Stay chill,*" Raven warned him. "*We're not out of the woods yet.*"

"What did you want me to do?" Drow asked her.

"*Proceed as planned to the rendezvous at the*

Space Operations Center," Raven told him. *"Gift and Tally will be arriving early this evening on a stratojet which gets in at 1800 hours. Assuming we succeed as planned, we'll arrange for you to return to the airport and escort them to the pre-arranged meeting place. Do you understand?"*

"Yes," Drow assured her. "And . . . ?"

"Yes?"

"Thank you. I owe you."

"Don't consider it a debt," the Hex said. *"This is what gives me a buzz."*

And with that she was gone. Drow was unable to stop himself smiling. Not only was he relieved that Tally and Gift were safe, Raven's words had relieved his mind of another burden. The Hexes had told him something of their situation and the reason for this assault on the center of Federation power and it had seemed as if the outlook for them would be grim if this mission failed. But if Raven, heading into danger and uncertainty, could still find life exciting maybe things weren't as bad as they seemed. For the first time he wondered what the world would be like if the Hex cause succeeded.

Sergeant Crispian sat in the front of the flitter, watching the city flow past the windows as one of his men piloted the craft. Ahead of them the Space Operations Center was becoming visible. It was an impressive building, like all the buildings in Transcendence, reaching up in a slender point toward the sky. Crispian wondered why the two Intelligence Officers thought it might be vulnerable to terrorists. He couldn't imagine why terrorists would be interested in it. Space exploration was one of the lowest priorities of the European Federation. Scientific progress had been confined to the Earth for hundreds of years. Like genetic mutation, space exploration was an alarming and unpopular subject for science to explore. The current government, like all of its predecessors, wanted the human race to remain exactly what it was and where it was.

As the flitters approached the spire of the Space Operations Center, Crispian wondered to himself how such an unpopular field of research had gained a prized position in the most impressive city on Earth. Although he'd lived in Transcendence for almost six years he had never visited the center, even though sections of it were open to the public. He hoped that the Intelligence Officers wouldn't expect him to know the details of its operation. But they seemed unconcerned as the Seccie team formed itself into an escort around them.

"The main entrance is that way," the female Force Commander said authoritatively and her companion nodded.

"Shall we observe the museum first?" he asked.

"We may as well. Our brief is to study the facility in detail," she replied and Sergeant Crispian's squad fell into step behind them as they headed toward the arch of the entrance.

It didn't take long for the staff of the Space Center to realize they had important visitors. Professor Moore, the senior scientist in charge of the space project, hurried down to meet them as the two Commanders looked idly around the main foyer. Objects from the first European ventures into space had been displayed in glass cases around the room and the Intelligence Officers studied them with apparent interest as Moore told them how pleased he was to meet them.

"I had almost come to believe that the government didn't attach much importance to my work," he confessed. "I can't tell you how glad I am that you've come to inspect the Center. I only wish I'd had more time to prepare."

"Would you have time to prepare for a

terrorist attack, Professor?" the woman asked sharply, her black eyes studying him assessingly.

"No, Commander, I suppose not," Moore admitted.

"That is why you were not informed of our inspection," the white-haired man explained. "Now, to explain our wishes."

"Certainly, certainly," Moore said eagerly. "But first, may I offer you refreshment, anything—"

"Thank you, no," the man said firmly. "We will begin immediately, starting with the parts of the Center that are open to the public—the museum and the viewing gallery. We will then require an explanation of the operation of the private parts of the center, its security system and its computer database. Finally, we will inspect the specialized security system which controls the orbital satellite network. Is that possible?"

"Of course, Commander," Moore replied. "We will put ourselves entirely at your disposal." He glanced over at the squad of Seccies. "Will your men wait here?" he asked. "Would *they* like any refreshment?"

Sergeant Crispian doubted whether senior officers were likely to be at all concerned about his comfort but it seemed he had misjudged them. The female commander gave the squad a long look and then smiled.

"I believe they would, Professor," she said. "Perhaps one of your staff could conduct them to a private room to await us?"

"Anything you wish, Madam," the scientists said, clearly relieved to be able to offer someone something, and signaled to one of his assistants. As a polite young lady led Crispian and his men away, the Sergeant grinned at his squad. This was much more preferable to inspecting the IDs of an endless flow of tourists. He still had no idea why the officers could be bothered to inspect so unimportant a facility but, with a much-needed rest awaiting him, he couldn't bring himself to care.

Wraith was conscious of a genuine fascination as the senior scientists began his tour. The man was trying hard to be pleasant, despite a slight nervousness in the presence of the important guests he imagined they were, and his description of the history of space flight was more interesting than Wraith had imagined.

The ganger had never really thought much about the exploration of space. Like most people, he knew that it had been a prominent issue about three hundred years ago and that it had been more or less abandoned since. It had never occurred to him to wonder why. Now, as he studied the carefully preserved objects of a history of reaching into the unknown it occurred to him for the first time that space exploration had a important significance. To many of the citizens of the EF, trapped in misery or poverty, the simple idea of there being other worlds and other possibilities might have relieved some of the hopelessness of their situation. He had lived all his life with people who genuinely believed that the world would never change. But space exploration was a field of science full of potential new discoveries. Every word the Professor said confirmed that.

"Of course we have only a limited budget," he was explaining. "Cuts in funding over the past few years have meant that we've had to scale down several of our projects. But the museum brings in extra revenue and, I assure you, Commanders, we keep the public carefully isolated from the most sensitive areas." He paused, as a group of tourists entered the museum and, lowering his voice, asked, "Would you like these people removed while you make your inspection? We can easily close the public parts of the building for a short while."

"There's no need," Wraith told him. "We prefer to observe the building as it is normally used."

Raven said nothing, but her eyes flickered briefly across to the tourists and she smiled to herself. Alaric and Jordan were doing an excellent job of examining the exhibits with a slightly bored expression and Luciel and Kez had equipped themselves with data-pads and were making a more careful inspection and taking notes as they did so. Drow looked somewhat out of place but, although he ignored some exhibits entirely and studied others with an obvious interest, Raven didn't think his behavior was out of character for a tourist.

As Professor Moore moved on, lovingly describing the exhibits and how they came to be there, Raven found herself regretting what would become of this building. But, she thought to herself, it was fitting for this collection of dusty memorabilia to disappear from view forever. Although the Professor cared deeply for the objects in his custody, the EF had entombed the study of space in this building. The friendly scientist had refused to accept it but the government had no interest in aiding his research.

Sergei Sanatos stared glumly out of the window of his splendid apartments in the Palace of Versailles. At a meeting that morning his officials had informed him that the quest for the rogue Hex could not continue much longer. All over Europe Security Service operatives had been pulled from their jobs in order to aid the CPS with the quest. Every department in the massive EF bureaucracy was helping with the search. The elderly Minister of Propaganda had given up every last drop of information he recalled about the previous Hex threat and the Minister of Internal Affairs had locked down the entire city of Padua on the basis of a thread of information about two of Theo Freedom's possible descendants. Nothing had done any good. The Hex was still at large and the President was running out of time and options.

Angrily Sanatos drummed his fingers on the window sill. He found it a source of immense frustration that his enemies were using the net against him. His ancestors had been fools and traitors to introduce the Hex mutation into the populace. He knew the secret that had been hidden from the citizens of the Federation for hundreds of years. The Hex gene was a true virus. It had seeded itself in the genetic code of people throughout the world. In only a few was it truly active but there were hundreds of thousands, maybe even millions, of people who had the potential to become Hexes. Now, it seemed, all it required was for a

Hex to rediscover the information Theo Freedom had learned, the secrets of how to unlock a Hex's potential, and then there would be anarchy. A nation of Hexes would be a nation of data thieves, privacy would disappear, politicians could be held truly accountable for their actions. Sanatos' hand clenched into a fist and he slammed it down with a crash. The Hex must be caught at all costs.

Striding across the room he tapped a familiar key combination into his personal vidcom and waited impatiently for the face of Joseph Levi, Minister of Technology, to appear on the screen. When it appeared, Joseph looked surprised but he smiled affably at the President.

"How may I help you, your Excellency?" he asked.

"I want a net search," Sergei barked. "I want you to devote all available computing resources to finding this Hex. I want you to scan the entire net for her identity. We have pictures of her, we have her DNA code, her precise genetic map. I want every security system in Europe scanning for her. No matter what it takes."

The Minister of Technology blanched.

"Sir," he said uneasily. "To initiate a network search of that magnitude would require all the computing power at our disposal. We would be able to carry out very few other tasks while it was in progress. The EF will be crippled while we look for this Hex."

"Were you not listening to me?" Sergei demanded. "Are you deaf? Have you suddenly become terminally stupid? Did you not hear me say that I didn't care what was necessary? I want the Hex, do you understand?"

"Yes, Sir," the Minister bowed his head. "I understand."

"Then do as I say," Sergei thundered and snapped the connection shut.

At the other end of the vidcom line, Joseph Levi let his breath out in a great gust. He had never seen the President in such a towering rage. Joseph had grave misgivings about devoting so many system resources of the net to the search for the Hex but he had no choice. Ponderously he reached for the keypad of his vidcom unit to issue the orders the President had given him.

Inside the computer network small subroutines fired up and passed their commands to insignificant applications, those applications passed on their information to larger programs and those programs began to construct huge, wide-ranging search parameters. Gradually the flow of data through the net slowed as more and more resources committed themselves. Terminals across Europe suddenly began to run at half the speed as the net began its quest for Raven.

But as the dataflow slowed something gathered strength. With every encumbered connection, every delayed access request, the cloud of darkness grew larger. Tendrils of blackness began to snake their way across the net. The city of light still caused it pain but in the depths of its dim consciousness it was becoming aware that the light was telling it something important, was searching for something that the darkness craved.

> RAVEN? < it asked, over and over and over again. It was a name the darkness knew, a name that gave its hate form. Gradually it gathered itself and, wherever the light searched for the thing named Raven, the darkness followed it. And with every microsecond that passed the cloud grew in size and strength.

• • •

Professor Moore was coming to the end of his tour. The two Intelligence Officers had politely listened to his explanations with an attentiveness that gave him hope that maybe this time the government would change its mind. Every year he feared that the Center would be closed but perhaps his fears had been in vain. Certainly he had nothing to be ashamed of in his work for the center. Every piece of equipment had been treasured and lovingly cared for. The security system was constantly manned, the computer network protected from hackers by its separation from the EF computer network and his staff dedicated and loyal. He assured the Commander with the cropped albino hair of this as his companion inspected the computer system.

"I'm sure you have done your duty, Professor," the Commander said politely. But it was clear that most of his attention was taken up by his colleague whose fingers flew across the keypad as she investigated every last scrap of data in the computer system.

"I assure you, everything is in order," the Professor said with concern as the woman finally turned away from the terminal and rose from her seat.

"As you say, Professor," she said with a slight smile. "Everything is in order." She glanced at the other officer. "It only remains for us to inspect the system which controls the orbital satellite network. Then our duties here are complete."

"Very well," Professor Moore nodded amicably. "If you would be so kind as to follow me?"

Raven's fingertips tingled in anticipation as the scientist led them to a separate control room. She could feel the system already, calling to her with promises of power and control. From within that system the net would be hers. She would take it and own it and no force the EF possessed could wrest it from her. Downstairs the other members of the Ghost team were already placing the explosive devices that would bury these computer terminals with the rest of the Space Center under tons of rubble. By the time the twisted blackened hulls of the computers which now awaited her so enticingly had been unearthed from the wreckage it would be too late for the EF to reclaim the satellites. They, and the net, would obey only her commands.

As they entered the satellite control room Raven glanced at Wraith and raised an eyebrow. He nodded imperceptibly and turned to the scientist.

"Thank you, Professor," he said smoothly. "You've been most helpful and

I'm certain this system will prove in as admirable condition as the last."

"I certainly hope so," Professor Moore replied, looking anxiously at Raven. "We realize how important the satellites are to the information network although we have many other projects which are of greater significance to the space program—"

"Indeed," Wraith replied with a smile. "In fact, while my colleague inspects the system, perhaps you would like to tell me about some of them in greater detail. I think that the refreshment you offered earlier might now be appropriate."

"Oh, of course," Professor Moore beamed at him. "I'd be delighted." He turned to Raven with an anxious expression. "I hope you don't mind us leaving you, Commander Wing? I can arrange for one of my assistants to attend you, if you wish?"

"There's no need, Professor," Raven replied, seating herself in front of the terminals. "This shouldn't take me long. I'll join you shortly."

"Very well then," Professor Moore bowed in acquiescence and turned back to Wraith. "If you'll be so good as to come with me, Commander?"

They left the room together and Raven could hear the Professor expounding on his pet projects as they headed down the corridor. She grinned fiendishly. Before her lay the brain of the orbital satellite network, exposed and unguarded. The mission had proceeded even more smoothly than they had hoped. Laying her hands on the keypad of the terminal, Raven plunged into the system.

The password protocols of the satellite network had been safely constructed to foil attempts by hackers or spies to subvert them. For microseconds Raven hung at the edge of the system, observing the security subroutines clustering like a pack of wolves around the edge of the system, keeping her from the chained gates that led inside. Then, carefully, she moved forward. One of the subroutines saw her and rushed forward to meet her.

> **who you?** < it demanded, sniffing her suspiciously.

Raven reached down to touch it, sending a sequence of commands that would soothe its suspicions.

> **a friend** < she told it. > **be calm** <

Another one noticed her and began to clamor for more information.

> **password! password! password!** < it demanded, its yelps attracting the rest of the pack.

She reached out to it and examined its design, using its behavior as a clue to what the password might be. She remained touching it for a few more microseconds until her mind located in its programming the unique phrase which would render it dormant.

> **through adversity to the stars** < she informed it and the subroutine lay down at her feet, satisfied.

The rest of the pack of subroutines was approaching now, yapping more inquiries.

> **identity!** < they demanded. > **system user protocol!—purpose of interface!— security code!** <

Raven could have worked out the answers to their questions but instead she adopted a simpler method. Reaching down to the two subroutines she had already reassured, she pointed them toward their fellows.

> **reassure them** < she ordered.

The subroutines hastened back to the back and rubbed themselves against their fellows, touching tails and noses sociably.

> **no trouble here** < they barked. > **relax—relax—return to posts** <

Following them, Raven moved through the pack to the entrance of the system. As she passed she touched other pack members lightly and, tamed by her now familiar scent, they clustered about her slavishly. Programmed to recognize the pack's satisfaction, the great gates swung open and Raven passed within.

The system was ancient, designed long ago and never upgraded to keep it in tune with developments in the net. But Professor Moore had cared for it rigorously and every data file was as perfectly formatted as the day it had been introduced into the system. Streams of commands flowed through it, informing the five hundred and twenty-three satellites currently in orbit of what their duties were. For the most part these commands were simple, dictating the patterns of their journeys around the world, but within the stream of code was one significant section. It informed the satellites who they belonged to and who had authority to change their orders.

>**display full security parameters**< Raven ordered the system and examined the code. It was complex, allowing for any number of specialized circumstances in which the EF government could use the satellites to control the flow of data through the net.

> **erase parameters** < Raven ordered and the stream of code vanished. Now the satellites were free agents, passing data across the net without priority or prejudice.

> **save new parameters** < Raven told the system and listed the names of its new masters. > **raven—ali—luciel—avalon—wraith—kez—alaric—geraint—jordan—cloud. require authorization from named**

users for future changes. < Deciding that was sufficient, she turned her attention to a new file.

> **display restrictions on access** < she commanded and an immense stream of code fell into her hands.

The EF had made the network their tool and the orbital satellite system was the whip they used to control it. The satellites had been ordered to hold back all transmissions that contained key phrases the Federation had flagged as seditious, all transmissions emanating from locations the EF believed to be controlled by dissidents and all information that could possibly be used against them. Raven smiled as she ordered the satellites to erase those restrictions and inserted her own.

> **refuse transmissions from all Security Services agents+operatives past/present/future** < she began. > **refuse transmissions from all CPS agents+operatives past/present/future—refuse transmissions of arrest warrants/censorship/government directives —refuse all EF orders relating to the capture of criminals/subversives/mutants** <

> **request authorization?** < the system asked, obedient to her previous commands, and Raven smiled to herself.

> **authorization *raven*** < she confirmed and the system hastened to obey her.

11

Loose the Seven Seals

The terminal screen went dark. The Minister for Technology, Joseph Levi, tapped the key combination to bring it to life. Nothing happened. Irritated now, he keyed in another combination intended to be used in the event of a system crash. Again nothing happened. He frowned and turned to the vidcom unit, intending to summon a subordinate to address the problem, and tapped in a call-code. The vidcom unit failed to respond.

Levi got up from his desk and went to the door of his study. It slid open to reveal his outer office, normally filled with assistants quietly performing the tasks he had set them. Now it was a scene of chaos. All over the room the screens had blacked out and men and women frantically tapped in a series of combinations on to their unresponsive keypads. It took a few minutes for one of his assistants to notice him standing there. Finally one of them turned and saw him.

"Minister!" she exclaimed, and the other occupants of the room turned to regard him.

"What's going on?" Levi demanded. "Is there a problem with the system?"

"I think it might be a problem with the network, Sir," the woman who had first observed him responded. "Nothing seems to be working. I've tried everything I can think of."

"So have I," a young man added, not looking up from the terminal into which he continued to key useless codes. "I've used all the security passwords for my clearance level. Nothing seems to work."

"Perhaps your clearance, Minister?" the woman asked hopefully and Levi nodded curtly.

Crossing to the nearest terminal, he ordered his subordinates to look away as he typed in the highest security clearance passwords, known only to him and the President. The screen stayed dark. He sat back from the screen and thought for a while. Then, turning back to his assistants, he ordered:

"Close down our connection to the network and restart the terminals."

Everyone in the office held their breath as the young man manually adjusted the setting of the main server connection. Then they heaved a communal sigh of relief as the terminal screens brightened again.

"Don't relax yet," Levi warned. "This only means our computer system is still working. We still don't have net access." He looked quickly around the room and gestured to his assistants one by one. "You, go and get a report from the technicians at the Versailles Computer Complex, you'll have to take a flitter since the vidcoms aren't working. You, visit every office and department in this building, find out how many of them, if any, still have net access and inform the others to close their net connections until the problem had been isolated. You, go and take a message to the office of the President and inform his Excellency of what has occurred here. You, summon two additional detachments of troops to guard this building; this may be the initial strike of a terrorist attack."

He paused for breath as his subordinates scuttled to do his bidding. He was sweating and breathing heavily and he felt nauseous.

"What can be the meaning of this?" he asked quietly to himself.

"Minister?" one of his assistants interrupted his musings.

"Yes?" he replied sharply, annoyed at the interruption.

"Minister, just before the crash, my terminal had reported a result on that search you requested," the man said diffidently. "I don't know if it's relevant but—"

"Search," Levi frowned to himself then his eyes brightened. "The search for the Hex?" He hurried over to the terminal in question and stared at it. "Show me the result!"

Fumbling with the keypad the assistant produced the last screen of information he had seen before the crash. Words formed on the screen and then an image was produced beneath them.

> **Security vidcam (no.#2356346567) in Transcendence, Unity district, captured image (rendered on screen) at 1600 hours today. Correlation with subject "Raven." Probability 97%. <**

The Minister and his assistant gazed at the image. It was a young woman. She was dressed in a heavy black greatcoat which swung open slightly to reveal a military uniform. She had black hair, braided in accordance with military regulations into a long plait, and her eyes were dark and secretive.

Levi stared at it, transfixed. He wondered if it was actually possible that the President's last-ditch attempt to locate the renegade Hex had actually succeeded. Then suddenly he stiffened.

"What uniform is that?" he demanded.

The assistant whose terminal it was shrugged and looked embarrassed.

"Not sure, Sir," he admitted. "I'm not aware of all the grades and you can't see very much—"

"No excuses," Levi snarled. He looked wildly across the room. "You!" He beckoned urgently. "What uniform is that?"

Lieutenant Armitage, the Seccie assigned to him as a personal bodyguard, hurried across the room and came to look at the screen. Unhesitatingly he answered.

"Military Intelligence, Sir," he said quickly. "And the tags are those of a Force Commander."

"A Force Commander?" the Minister's voice rose to a yell. "There's a Hex in Transcendence wearing a Force Commander's uniform? How is that even possible?"

Everyone turned to look at him, the horror on their faces a mirror of his.

"Get in touch with Transcendence Military Command!" Levi shouted. "Now! I don't care how you do it. Give them that picture and tell them to capture that woman at all costs."

"Yes, Sir," the Seccie guard replied, snapping to attention. Then he raced out of the room as if the fires of hell were at his back.

"Then get me Alverstead," Levi continued, still trembling with emotion. "The head of the CPS. I want him to identify this woman. He's the only one who's met this Hex. Maybe it isn't her."

Another assistant left to find the CPS Governor and the Minister sank into the nearest chair. He hoped against hope that the computer system's probability estimate was incorrect. But he doubted it would be. Somehow, against all possibility, a Hex had managed to infiltrate one of the most powerful strongholds of the Federation. By now she could be wreaking untold havoc with her stolen military authority. Levi shook his head silently as he catalogued the powers an Intelligence Division Force Commander had. She could order almost anything in that uniform. Only a tactical nuclear strike required a higher clearance.

Levi felt the rule of the EF crumbling around him. They had lost control of the net. The rogue Hex was working against them in a city she should not have been able to come within a hundred miles of. Somewhere other Hexes concealed a disk which would unlock their true potential. The Pres-

ident of the Federation was a man obsessed.
He had ordered Raven's capture at any cost
while the Federation rocked on its foundations. Levi suspected that the troops stationed in Transcendence were about to fight
the last battle of a war which had already
been lost.

Sergeant Crispian sipped his second cup
of coffee, slowly savoring the bitter taste.
His men were wolfing down the plates of
delicacies the Space Center's staff had pro-
vided but, for now, Crispian was content
just to get the weight off his feet. He was
amused by the eagerness with which the
Center staff were serving his squad. Perhaps he should have visited his facility
before, he wondered. The people here had
been neglected by the important powers of
the Federation for so long that they were
prepared to go to any lengths to impress the
Intelligence Officers. That including hosting
Crispian's squad in luxurious comfort.
Crispian stretched out his legs and
leaned back in the comfortable chair, wondering if it would be inappropriate to have
a brief nap while he was waiting for the officers to return. He lifted the cup of coffee to
his lips once more and then, with a start,
spilled the remaining hot liquid across his

legs. He jumped to his feet with a curse. A loud alarm was going off, almost deafening him with its siren blaring.

"What the hell is that?" he demanded.

"Evacuation alarm," the pretty young girl who'd been serving them drinks said fearfully. "We must leave the building at once."

"Why?" Crispian asked anxiously. "What would trigger the alarm?"

"I've never heard it before," the girl told him. "But it's supposed to go off in the event of a fire or if the security system detects an explosive device."

"An explosive device?" Crispian signaled to his men and they headed for the door, the girl running to keep up with them. "There are two Intelligence Officers assessing your facility for vulnerability to terrorists. I hope for your sake they don't end up being blown up in the middle of their inspection."

Jordan waited impatiently in the pilot's seat of the skimmer. Kez and Luciel sat in the back, surreptitiously clutching their guns. The weapons had been coated with a material to render them invisible to the scanning devices of Transcendence but Raven had warned them to keep them out of sight of the vidcams. Alaric was standing at the skimmer door, holding his own gun in one of the deep pockets of his coat, watching for any sign of Raven, Wraith or the Seccie squad.

"I hope we set the timers right," Jordan fretted. "If Raven's injured I'll never forgive myself."

"She'll be chill," Kez said with an exaggerated confidence. "She always is."

"And the timers were fine," Drow said, speaking confidently despite his unfamiliarity with the other Ghosts. "That tech was elite."

"There they are!" Luciel exclaimed and Jordan whirled back to look at the entrance of the Space Center.

A group of people were racing out of the building. Among the scientists and Seccie guards Raven was instantly recognizable, her flag of long black hair flying loose and her long coat flapping like wings behind her. Wraith was keeping pace with her and the two of them were outdistancing the Seccie squad who hadn't yet realized that the "officers" were heading in a slightly different direction from them.

"Over here," Alaric called, waved wildly with his free hand, and the leader of the Seccie squad glanced over at him. The man's mouth dropped open in amazement as he saw that the two Force Commanders, whose orders he had been unquestioningly following, were racing for the skimmer.

As Raven and Wraith threw themselves inside the vehicle Jordan heard a dull thunder noise. Alaric fell in after them and slammed the door shut as there was a second thundering boom and the Space Operations Center began to cave in on itself. The Seccie squad leader was still staring, openmouthed, as Jordan gunned the engine of the skimmer and sped away from the collapsing building as fast as she could.

As the skimmer raced through the city toward the rendezvous point Jordan didn't need to ask if Raven had been successful. The city was in uproar. Seccie flitters were everywhere, racing past the elegant pinnacles and minarets of Transencdence's sculpted buildings with their sirens wailing. Crowds of people milled about in the street, still not entirely aware of what had occurred. Jordan doubted that the collapse of the Space Operations Center would even be noticed in the hubbub.

"This is unprecedented," Alaric said, looking at the city as they skimmed through the crowded streets. "It looks like a broken ant's nest."

"Isn't it one?" Raven said with a faint laugh from where she lay back, regarding the confusion passively from the window of the skimmer.

"It worked then," Luciel asked needlessly. "Everything went as planned?"

"Even better than planned," Wraith assured him.

"We still have to get out of this mess," Jordan pointed out, wrenching the controls to avoid a Seccie skimmer abandoned for some reason in the middle of the roadway. "Think your uniforms will buy us passage?"

"I wouldn't rely on it," Raven informed her. "Too risky."

"Let's just get to the rendezvous point and lie low for a while," Alaric recommended. "Then we'll see if Force Commanders Barrow and Wing have had their identities compromised."

"First we have to let Drow off," Jordan pointed out. "To collect Gift and Tally."

"I'm not certain he should go alone," Wraith said seriously but Drow shook his head.

"No," he contradicted. "I can do this. The rest of you could be recognized by the Seccies, they have your descriptions on file. Gift and Tally are my responsibility first. Trust me not to fail them."

Alaric nodded to himself and Kez grinned at Drow.

"Good luck then," Wraith said, accepting the inevitable, but Raven raised an eyebrow.

"Luck?" she asked. "This isn't luck. Destiny is on our side now."

There was in fact only one Force Commander in Transcendence. His name was Seiben Winter and he commanded five divisions of Federation Troops. He fitted almost exactly Sergeant Crispian's idea of a Military Intelligence Officer. For thirty years he had worked for the Federation and during that time he had followed orders scrupulously, even when those orders involved the torture and murder of rebels working against the interests of the government. He remembered the names of every last one of those victims of EF justice. A man with no illusions as to who or what he was, Commander Winter was nevertheless respected by the men under his command. Now his aide stood beside him with lowered eyes waiting for the Force Commander's decision.

"The order came through unconventional channels," Winter mused.

"Yes, Force Commander," the aide replied.

"You were unable to authenticate it

because of the network's failure to respond to our passwords."

"Yes, Commander."

"In which case it is possible our orders are not genuine," the Force Commander mused and his aide nodded. Winter remained silent for a while. When he spoke again it was in a strange tone of voice.

"I would have your opinion, Craddock," he told his aide.

"Yessir."

"We know that the net has been disrupted by a force unknown," the Commander began. "Possibly as a prelude to a devastating system crash. Our only source of information are the media broadcasts. However, I have had to order my men not to watch these because of the almost certainly illegal and seditious information they are broadcasting."

"Yessir."

"These reports from the media indicate the following," the Force Commander continued. "That the city of London is in a state of chaos. That President Sanatos has fled the palace Versailles with a fortune in gold bullion and his whereabouts are currently unknown. That all over the Federation riots are breaking out; triggered most probably by rumors that the Security Services have been crippled by the loss of the net. These riots are likely to lead to revolution since almost all the Federation troops are similarly crippled." He looked levelly at the aide. "In short we are facing the complete breakdown of our civilization."

"So it would appear, Sir," Craddock replied. An exemplary soldier, he didn't break his position although a twitch at the corner of his mouth betrayed his anxiety.

"With this in mind, Craddock," Commander Winter went on. "And think carefully, bearing in mind that we are honor-bound to obey any legitimate order we receive. Does it seem likely to you that the Military Command would order what are possibly the last five active and operational troop divisions in Europe to search the city for a young female Hex and have her eliminated?"

The aide's face was studiedly blank. Craddock had served Commander Winter for twenty years. Throughout that time they had both followed every order they had received, believing unquestioningly in the rule of law. Now they had received what would possibly be their last order ever. That is, if it was genuine.

"Well, Craddock?" Commander Winter asked. "Does it seem likely to you that Military Command would give such an order?"

"Yes, Sir," the aide replied. "It does."

The Commander nodded.

"I agree with your assessment," he replied. "It is unquestioningly the most ludicrous and futile order I have ever received. It will almost certainly prove impossible to carry out and, if we should succeed, will not do one iota of good in limiting the chaos that is now upon us."

"Yessir."

"Nevertheless," Commander Winter concluded. "It is an order. Have the troops begin the search."

The crew of the stratojet hurried to fasten all the compartments and check that all the passengers were fastened into their seats. The pilot's voice was projected across the plane.

"Ladies and Gentlemen," it said, pretending to an unlikely confidence. *"A situation of possible emergency exists. We are experiencing some difficulties making contact with Transcendence air control. We are also experiencing some difficulties with our connection to the information network. Therefore, could all passengers please prepare for a possible crash landing. I repeat, a situation of possible emergency exists, could all passengers brace themselves for a crash landing."*

The auburn-haired boy in seat 16B,

whose name on the passenger list was given as Edward Anderson, turned to the person in the next seat and whispered:

"Is this something to do with us?"

"How should I know?" the girl replied equally quietly. Her name was officially Elsie Anderson and her similarity of features to the boy beside her identified her as his sister. "But I think it might be genuine. If we'd been identified they'd have stopped us during a routine check at the terminal, not faked a stratojet crash." She paled as she realized what she had just said. "Which means the jet *is* about to crash."

"Fasten your seat belt, Tally," her brother warned. "And brace yourself."

"What if we do crash?" she asked with a frightened look.

"Then the second they open the doors we slip out and find Drow. And if we can't find him we hide until we can." Gift looked grim. "Strange things are happening, Tally," he said softly. "I'm sure of it."

"Me too," his sister whispered and then she closed her eyes, burying her head in her arms as she prepared for a crash landing.

Similar events were occurring all over the Federation. The combination of the EF's commitment of all their system resources to finding Raven, the Federation's loss of the orbital satellite network and the increase in strength of the darkness of the net that had once been Kalden's mind had resulted in accidents and emergencies all across Europe. In England, the media channel Populix had resumed broadcasting to inform the people of London of what was going on. The other media channels across the Federation followed suit, providing the EF's citizens with their only information about a world becoming gradually insane.

But, despite the riots and revolutions beginning in many of the European cities, civilization had not completely broken down. In many places volunteers had stepped forward to rescue the victims of accidents caused by the failure of the net. In others citizens had disarmed the local Seccies and were taking the law into their own hands to protect and serve the population. In London, Geraint and Ali had organized the Ghosts into bands and were policing the streets. Their presence alone was controlling the rival gangs while the Seccies fled en masse from the area.

However, the decay of the information network continued. Too much had been asked of it in too short a time. It struggled sluggishly to continue the flow of data but was opposed by a dark and heavy force.

The remains of Kalden's mind exulted.
Everywhere the city of light was fading and
dying. The chattering data channels were
slowing and stopping, a flood becoming a
narrow stream and finally a pathetic trickle.
In the space the net had occupied the cloud
of darkness flowed unimpeded. Coiling
over and over itself it stretched its multiple
tentacles through the remains of the network. A mighty Kraken in an ocean of
thought, it lurked in the dark depths and
waited for its prey. At whatever point the
object of its hate entered the net, the darkness would be waiting to consume it.

Drow scanned the rushing crowds desperately. The chaos had begun gradually in
the airport as the terminals had darkened.
But, once it had begun, the panic spread
rapidly. Now people ran wildly hither and
thither, some carrying heavy luggage, others abandoning their possessions in their
urgency to get to safety. Three incoming
stratojets were reported to have crashed on
arrival but Drow couldn't get any sense out
of the staff who were frantically attempting
to get their useless computers back on line.
Something had gone badly wrong, the
young hacker realized—Raven's takeover
of the satellite network had not been

intended to have these effects. He had an
ominous feeling on the confusion and misery that surrounded him now and shuddered.

He walked on, trying not to let the
passersby jostle him too much in their
flight. Somewhere in this terminal were Gift
and Talent. He had let them down once
before, giving them advice that might have
led to their deaths; he was determined not
to do so again. If they were here, he would
find them. He continued to scan the crowds,
uselessly. There were children of all ages
everywhere, some crying pathetically, separated from their parents. None of them
looked like the ones he was looking for.
Drow's heart was racing and he could feel
his own fear like a physical pain, tight and
sharp in his chest. He willed himself to calm
down and wondered what one of he Ghosts
would do in his place. Even without the net
to help her, someone like Raven would have
thought of something.

Suddenly he remembered something Ali
had told him back in the Ghost enclave in
London.

"Raven recognized Avalon," she had
said. "She knew the first time she saw her
that she was a Hex. She knew when she met
me for the first time as well. There's something about us she can recognize."

It was an ability Ali had admitted she herself did not possess but nonetheless it was possible. Drow had touched Tally and Gift's minds. More than that, he had virtually touched their souls. He knew that when he saw them he would recognize them immediately. Of that he was certain. The only problem was finding them.

He stopped stock-still and closed his eyes. People slammed into him and swore as he got in their way. He ignored them, concentrating. Somewhere in all this confusion Tally and Gift were looking for him. Without him they had no one to protect them and nowhere to go. With every fiber of his mind he strained toward them. Filling his mind with all his hope and desperation he reached out. And connected.

Drow's eyes snapped open. There they were. Two small figures standing about thirty meters away by a graceful fluting pillar. They were looking around, holding each other's hands so as not to get separated. As he looked at them they turned, almost as one person, and their eyes met his. He felt a sudden grin break out on his face and in unison the twins smiled back. Together they crossed the terminal to meet each other and within minutes came face to face.

"I found you," Drow said. "Despite everything."

"I was sure you would," Gift replied, grinning back.

"I wasn't," Tally admitted. "But I'm glad you did."

"We'd better get out of here," Drow told them. "Everything's on the fritz. The net seems to have gone down."

"Where to?" Gift asked. "What's the plan?"

"There's a rendezvous point," Drow explained. "The others are waiting for us there."

"Then let's go," Tally said quickly and they headed for the exit.

"We should hurry," Gift said as they forced their way through the crowds. "There's something we didn't tell you before."

"What's that?"

"We have a disk," Tally explained. "It's the only copy that exists. But the information on it is incredibly important to our kind of people." She looked around her at the frantic crowds. "Whatever's going on," she said, "maybe the information we have can stop it."

Raven was the first to realize that something was wrong. The others, elated by their success, were chattering eagerly as Jordan expertly navigated the skimmer through the city. But Raven, watching the movement of the crowds and activities of the Seccie flitters, remained silent. At the back of her mind there was a nagging doubt. The darkness in the net had been growing slowly. In her assessment the rate of its development had not been fast enough for it to have become a serious threat. And yet the chaos in the streets was increasing. Transcendence was a bastion of EF power. It should have been one of the last places to be affected by her appropriation of the satellite network. But the city was falling apart before her eyes and she wondered if she had made a tactical error. It was possible that recent events had changed the growth rate of Kalden's shattered mentality. If that was the case they might be in serious trouble.

Raven reached forward and touched Jordan's arm to get her attention. The girl glanced back at her with a quick smile.

"What is it, Raven?" she asked easily. "Something up?"

"Something's wrong," Raven said softly and the others fell silent. "Speed up," she continued. "I should get to a terminal as soon as possible. I think we might be in trouble."

The humming of the skimmer's engines changed note and became a low whine as

Jordan coaxed every last atom of power from the vehicle. No one said a word as they swept on through the city. Raven's words had disturbed their mood of euphoria and now each of them felt the tension in the air. No one countered her assertion that something was wrong.

It seemed half a hundred years until Jordan stopped the skimmer with a skid in the forecourt of a huge hotel. There was no one on duty at the desk as they entered but that didn't stop them. They took the lift, miraculously still working, to the rooms they had booked the night before. When they got there Kez produced a set of tools from his coat and efficiently picked the lock. Alaric and Jordan stood guard duty in case they were disturbed. Raven waited in silence and Luciel and Wraith watched her. Her face was expressionless but her pupils were dilated, a response that in anyone else they would have identified as fear.

The door opened and they entered the suite. Raven spotted the terminal immediately and crossed the room toward it even as Kez was carefully shutting the door behind them. Without a word she rested her hands on the keypad and immediately gave a soft gasp. Then she was still, a statue carved in ivory and obsidian, as her eyes glazed over in communion with the network.

12

Alpha and Omega

It had seemed to Raven that the net had been with her all her life. In the asylum blockhouse where she had grown up it had been her only real sanctuary, whispering secrets to her from another world. For years she had only really felt alive when her fingers touched the keypad of a terminal and her mind melded with the net to become her true self. Inside the network she became the legend others saw her as. Even when Kalden had experimented on her she had been able to reach out to the pathways of the net and draw them to herself. Never had she been unable to reach the infinite city of light.

Now she fell into darkness. It seemed unimaginably far. She fell as if in a dream and could not stop herself. Nowhere around her could she find the network. The last time she had faced this darkness she had been armed in light. Now there was no light to find. Instead the darkness spoke to her.

> **Raven** < it said. > **I begin to remember** <

Force Commander Sieben Winter watched the rioters in the streets from the armored military flitter. His aide, Craddock, was piloting, keeping the vehicle well above the raging crowds.

"It is anarchy," Commander Winter said. His voice was calm but his eyes were angry. Craddock didn't answer him. In all the years he had served with the Force Commander he had known him for a dangerous man. He had killed ruthlessly and tortured without mercy. But unlike other military officers, especially those in the Intelligence Division, he had never shown any pleasure in his actions. He had seemed more like a robot than a man, dedicated to performing his duties with every fraction of his being. Craddock feared his Commander's anger but trusted his judgement implicitly. There were few soldiers, even among the officers, that the aide admired. But Commander Winter could be relied upon and there was nothing more likely to gain Craddock's respect.

The Commander's com unit chimed, not needing a link to the network to perform its functions, and he answered it.

"Winter, here," he said precisely, and waited.

Craddock couldn't hear what was said on the other end of the signal but he saw the Force Commander's eyes change. He looked almost regretful but when answered he sounded as efficient as ever.

"Surround the building," he said. "I will be there directly."

Closing the connection, he turned to his aide.

"A Seccie squad has reported," he said. "While fleeing the devastation of the city they observed a group of people, two in uniforms of Force Commanders, entering a hotel in the Serendipity district. One of the uniformed officers was female and had long black hair."

"That is the description we received of the Hex, Sir."

"Correct," the Commander replied. "Accordingly we will proceed to this hotel, the Gardenia, in the Serendipity district. Then we will enter the building and eliminate the Hex in accordance with our orders."

"Yessir," Craddock said and touched the controls of the flitter directing it toward the district of the city the Commander had named. He glanced sideways at his superior officer and coughed to attract his attention. "Sir?" he asked.

"Yes, Craddock?" The Commander looked surprised to hear his aide speak, as well he might seeing as his orders had been easy to understand.

"May I ask a question, Sir?" Craddock asked.

"You may."

"What about after we've apprehended the Hex, Sir?" the aide asked apologetically. "What do we do then?"

The Force Commander thought for a while before speaking. Finally he answered.

"Well, Craddock," he said. "Seeing as the world we know is ending, in the circumstances I believe it would be appropriate for you to take some leave."

"Yessir, thank you, Sir," Craddock replied. "If I may ask another question, Sir?"

"Yes?"

"What will you be doing, Commander?"

Commander Winter looked surprised.

"I shall stand duty and await orders, of course," he said.

• • •

In London three children were also standing duty. Cara and Lucy were veterans of the Hex cause and had lived among the Ghosts ever since being rescued from extermination or worse. Charis was a newcomer who barely understood the controls of the laser pistol she was holding. But all three were loyal to their charge. They stood outside a building in the Ghost enclave waiting for Ali to join them. Since the decision to attack, it had been agreed that none of the senior Ghosts should travel anywhere without an escort.

"But I'm still not sure why I was assigned," Charis was saying. "I don't know anything about weapons or fighting."

"You'll learn," Lucy assured her. "We all did."

"If she has the time," Cara pointed out. "I mean, I don't want to sound weird but it looks as if everything's happening right now."

"You're right," Lucy agreed. "Charis, we should probably try to teach you a little more now."

"Don't look so worried," Cara added. "I know why you're here even if you don't. Ali must want to keep an eye on you. I heard Raven telling her you had a lot of potential and she should know. She's the best there is."

"Really?" Charis's expression was doubtful. She was dubious of the wild-looking Hex who ad appeared so alarmingly in her parent's apartment. "Ali impressed me more."

"You're skitzo!" Cara exclaimed. "I mean, Ali's a good leader, but Raven is . . ." She shook her head, at a loss of words.

"Ignore her," Lucy advised the new recruit. "It's getting to be like the cult of Raven around here. It's about time someone introduced some perspective."

Cara opened her mouth to object but she never said the words she had planned. Instead her eyes widened as she stared up through the levels.

"My God," she breathed quietly. "Look at that!"

The other two girls looked up automatically and stared, equally transfixed. Across the city lights were flashing, whole city blocks were darkening while in other areas lights flashed on and off too quickly to see other than as a blur.

"Something strange is happening," Lucy said, stating the obvious. "We should go get Ali."

"Tell her it looks like the net is crashing," Cara added.

"It is?" Charis's rapt gaze switched to the young Hex in alarm. "How?"

"I don't know." Cara looked back with a troubled expression. "But I've listened to stuff the older Ghosts have said about net crash. It looks to me as if this is it."

"But . . ." Lucy paused at the doorway, looking back at her friend. "What are we going to do?"

"Hey," Cara said suddenly, snapping back to reality. "Stop looking like the sky is falling. Even if it is that's no reason to fall apart. We've trained for this, you know we have. This is why we were taught to use weapons, this is why we were taught to be Hexes. This is the moment we've been waiting for. It's no use being scared of it. We're supposed to be fighting a war, remember? Now go and tell our Commander the battle has begun."

Drow ran into the hotel, Gift and Tally following only paces behind him. The chaos in the streets was growing. They had had to avoid groups of rioters, smashing into buildings to look what lay inside, more than once as they headed for the rendezvous. Drow had stolen a flitter, believing they would be safer in the air than on the ground. Tally and Gift had sat in the front with him, crammed into the forward passenger seat, and watched out for Seccies.

They had seen a few but they hadn't been stopped by them. Drow was more worried about the Federation troops he saw everywhere. They moved purposefully through the city, carrying heavy blasters, but they made no attempt to stop the rioters or impose any other kind of order.

Flinging himself into the lift, Drow waited as Tally and Gift joined him then touched the keypad to take them to the seventh floor.

"Something's very wrong," Tally muttered to herself and Gift looked angry.

"It always is, Tally. Isn't it?" he said sharply and Drow glanced at him quickly. "She's always predicting doom and gloom," Gift said quickly, looking slightly embarrassed.

"Let's hope she's wrong," Drow replied, pacing in the small lift space like a caged animal. "But I have a feeling . . ."

The lift stopped and Drow looked out into the corridor. It was empty.

"Come on," he said and they headed out of the lift, Drow reading the suite numbers until he came to the correct one. He knocked on the door, three quick raps, and it opened immediately to reveal Alaric standing there holding a gun.

"Drow!" he exclaimed in relief. "Quick, come in, all of you."

As the twins followed Drow into the hotel suite, all the Ghosts except Kez turned to regard them. Wraith was the first to speak.

"Gift. Talent," he said. "I am immeasurably relieved to see you here. You've braved greater dangers than you should ever have had to face and done credit to your names."

Tally stared, wide-eyed, at the white-haired man in the military uniform, unable to speak. But Gift felt something inside him resonate at the stranger's words.

"Thank you, Sir," he said simply. "But I think you've put yourselves in even greater danger to help us."

"One of us has," a girl spoke and the twins looked at her. She didn't look much older than they were and she clung to the arm of the young man who had opened the door to them. "There's something wrong with Raven," she said.

"Raven?" Tally asked in a whisper. The name called out to her as the white-haired man's words had called to Gift.

"Raven," said a thin boy who stood nearby. "She's our hacker. The leader of us Hexes. She went into the net an hour ago and she hasn't come out. She hasn't even moved." He stepped aside so they could see and the twins drew in their breath sharply.

Across the room, before a computer terminal, were two figures. The boy sat on the floor. He was crying, soundlessly, but his eyes didn't blink or·waver from the girl sitting as still as a statue in front of the terminal. She was barely breathing. Her black eyes stared blankly in front of her. Her thin pale hands rested on the keypad in front of her. The terminal screen was blank.

The thin boy who had spoken before and stepped aside so they could see their leader spoke again.

"I'm the only other Hex here," he said. "I tried to go in after her. But I couldn't. There's nothing there. I couldn't find her. I couldn't find anything."

The twins looked at each other. Then Gift reached into an inside pocket and pulled out the data disk. He extended it to Wraith.

"Sir," he said carefully. "We have this. Our grandfather was a Hex and a scientist. He studied the Hex abilities and recorded everything he learned on this disk. The EF killed him and my father to get it. My mother died to protect it." He stopped for a moment to take a deep breath. "Tally and I don't even know what's on it," he said. "But maybe it can help Raven."

Wraith reached out to take the disk and opened his mouth to speak. But before he could say anything there was a loud booming noise, the sound of an announcing device being turned on. Then, outside the hotel, a voice thundered:

"Hexes," it said. *"This building is surrounded. There is no escape. Deliver the criminal named Raven to us for execution and the rest of you may live."*

Craddock watched the building anxiously. There was no immediate response to Commander Winter's announcement. He wondered if the Hexes inside understood that the Commander was speaking the truth. The troops had moved into position soundlessly, ringing the hotel in black-uniformed soldiers. Now they stood ready. In no direction was there any escape. The aide wondered if the Hexes would give themselves up. In the circumstances it would be suicide not to.

"It seems they are reluctant," Commander Winter said. He lifted the announcer a second time and spoke into it.

"Hexes," he said. *"We have enough firepower to destroy the building. But my orders only require the elimination of the Hex named Raven. Deliver her and you have my word you will live."*

There was another delay and Craddock watched the building carefully. Just when he thought the Commander's words would go unrecognized, a figure appeared on one of the elegant balconies of the upper floors of the hotel. It was holding a piece of white fabric, apparently a sheet or blanket, and the wind whipped it into a flag.

"It would appear they wish to parley, Sir," he said.

"So it would seem," the Force Commander returned. "It is pointless in the circumstances. But we have some leeway as to time." He raised the announcer again.

"If you are prepared to negotiate, approach the edge of the balcony and wait to be collected," Commander Winter announced and the figure followed his instructions. It had closed the door through which it had emerged and stood waiting.

The Force Commander signaled to one of his men and the soldier hastened to the nearby military flitter and climbed into the pilot's seat. In moments he was guiding the craft up to the balcony where the figure waited.

"Are we not to storm the building then, Sir?" Craddock asked deferentially.

"We almost certainly will, Craddock," the Commander replied. "But I am curious to see what this rebel has to say for himself. I would like to know his rationale for bringing about Armageddon."

Commander and aide waited as the flitter returned and touched down. The soldier who had been piloting it exited, saluted, and opened the door for the rebel to exit. It was a man with short-cropped white hair. He wore a Force Commander's uniform and he regarded Commander Winter levelly.

"I am prepared to negotiate," he said. "In private."

"Then negotiate," the Commander replied. "Your request for privacy has been evaluated and denied."

"Very well." The man seemed untroubled. "You may call me Wraith."

"I am Force Commander Sieben Winter," the Commander replied. "At present I hold the highest authority in this city, which is under martial law. I demand that you deliver the Hex named Raven to me for execution. Then you may depart with such companions as you possess."

"Are you aware, Force Commander," the man named Wraith began, "that the information network is about to experience a permanent systems crash?"

"I would estimate the likelihood of such an occurrence as high," the Commander agreed.

"Are you also aware of the result of such a crash?"

"I am," the Commander replied. "Moreover, I have been informed that you and your companions were responsible for this situation."

"You have been informed incorrectly," Wraith told him. "The instigator of the crash is one of your own operatives, a Federation scientist named Kalden."

"I fail to see how one scientist could engineer a disaster of such epic proportions," the Force Commander replied.

"The scientist in question has been believed dead for two years," Wraith returned. "The Hex you referred to earlier, my sister, Raven, thought that she had ended his life. However, this event occurred while he was conducting certain experiments on her. The experimental equipment preserved what remained of Kalden's mind in the network. He is insane."

"That would explain a great deal," the Force Commander replied. "I had wondered why a Hex would destroy the network. You have relieved my mind of its curiosity. Accordingly, will you deliver the Hex so that I may proceed in carrying out my duty?"

"The Hex Raven," the man called Wraith said, "is currently engaged in attempting to prevent the systems crash we spoke of earlier. In the circumstances, will you withdraw your request that we surrender her?"

"I fear I will be unable to do that," Commander Winter replied. "My orders clearly state that I am to apprehend and execute the Hex."

"Carrying out your orders won't improve the situation we find ourselves in," Wraith stated baldly. "Perhaps you should consider other options?"

"I would be willing to," the Force Commander told him. "Regrettably, there are none."

Raven hung suspended in the darkness. As yet there was no pain. But she knew that would come later as her mind became increasingly divorced from sensation. She had no idea how long she had hung there, entrapped and enfolded in the dark cloud of Kalden's mind.

> **You thought you could escape me.** < the darkness told her, its words echoing through her mind. > **You were incorrect. Now you will suffer as I have suffered. I am not what I was but there is enough of me to assure you of that. You will suffer an eternity for every second I have suffered.** <

Raven was silent and the darkness clenched tighter around her.

> Why do you not speak? < it demanded. > Do you fear to? <

> What is there to fear? < Raven replied, speaking directly into the heart of the darkness. > You are nothing. <

> I am PAIN! < the darkness roared, thrashing around her, its voice an agony beating into her brain. > I am TORMENT. I am DARKNESS. DEATH. THE HORRORS OF THE VOID. I AM YOUR NIGHTMARE. FEAR ME <

> You are Nothing. < Raven replied simply. > You have no life in you. Even if you kill me you will still be Dead. I have nightmares to give you life. <

"Perhaps there is an option," Wraith said. "Are you prepared to hear it?"

"I am prepared to listen," Force Commander Winter agreed.

"Orders may be suspended when your superiors change their mind," Wraith pointed out. "Isn't that correct?"

"They have been in the past," the Commander acknowledged. "However, in this instance that possibility is unlikely since my superiors have no way to contact me and no prospect of doing so in the future."

"It is my belief that your superiors no longer hold any form of authority," Wraith informed him. "The President has fled. The rule of the EF is over. Your government has fallen."

"You may be correct," the Force Commander replied. "It makes no difference. I have my orders."

"I have every expectation that a new government is about to be put in place," Wraith said. "A coup has been mounted. Power now rests with the Hexes since they alone control the net. The European Federation is being effectively held to ransom. It has the option of committing suicide and condemning its citizens to the chaos of a network crash. Or it may surrender."

He looked about the plaza at the troops, then back at the Force Commander.

"I am a representative of the new government of the Federation," he said. "I am accordingly your new superior officer. You and your men may surrender to me."

Drow carried the disk to the terminal. Outside everything seemed quiet. Whatever Wraith was doing it had bought them some time.

"Will she know it's there?" Tally asked anxiously.

"I don't know," Alaric answered her. "But I don't have any better ideas."

"Raven," Drow said quietly. "I hope this works." Then, with a quiet click, he slid the disk into the terminal slot.

The Force Commander regarded the man before him. He was serious. Outnumbered by over a hundred to one, he was genuinely requesting that they surrender to him. The Commander approved.

"I will require proof of your authority before I can take your orders," he told the man. "Do you have such proof?"

"Will demonstrating that the information network is completely in our power suffice?" Wraith asked.

"It would," the Force Commander agreed. "Do you have such proof?"

"The Hex Raven is currently preventing a complete systems crash of the network," Wraith said, as if he was only informing the Commander of this for the first time. "If you are prepared to wait for her to succeed I can then provide you with proof of our authority."

"If she fails I will have to take it that your authority is illegitimate," the Force Commander told him.

"In which case I will deliver my sister to you for execution," Wraith replied.

His heart ached as he said the words but

he knew that he was making the right bargain. If Raven failed it meant she was trapped in the network forever, effectively dead anyway. Furthermore, if she failed, civilization would crumble. They would all die anyway. Everything depended on Raven now. But then, he thought to himself, it always had.

"That would be satisfactory," the Commander told him. "We will wait."

They stood together and waited for the end or the beginning of the world. Around them the lights were still going out. The city of artifice was failing as it lost its power. All over Europe the lights were going out and citizens of the Federation waited in darkness to discover what would become of them.

Something flickered at he edge of Raven's consciousness. A whisper of a memory of a thought. The darkness was still ranting and raving, ordering her to quail about it. Raven ignored it. It wanted her fear. Just as it had when it was Kalden, it wanted her to run screaming from it. But Raven had lived with fear all her life. She might be alone in the darkness but she had been alone and in the dark for most of her life. Ever since the death of her parents she had been alone. Only in the net was she alive. Being alone and in pain had become a part of her nature. She had refused to surrender to the darkness every day of her life. She would not surrender to fear now.

> **FEAR ME** < the darkness roared.

> **no** < she informed it.

It howled with rage, whirling around and about in the heart of itself. Everywhere was pain. Every thought in her mind was an agony. She ignored it.

The flicker came again and this time Raven reached for it. Any thought right now would distract her from the torment the darkness was holding her in. She reached for it and it burst into her brain, a torrent of information, a stream of words and thoughts. Every phrase glowed with light.

> **The Freedom Files** <

The darkness hesitated. Then it flinched. Light was pouring out of Raven and into the net. From the very heart of the black cloud she was emanating a flood of data, rebuilding the net out of her own essence with the flow of thought as her guide.

Deliberately she spoke the words that had been kept secret for twenty-five years, the truth that had waited to be heard ever since the Hex gene had first been discovered. These were the words which had explained to Raven the mystery of her own existence, clarifying everything she knew in one burst of illuminating freedom.

> The HEX gene is a discovery unparalleled in the history of human evolution. The melding of mind and machine is a development that has awaited the human race since its creation. To the HEX no space is a void. The universe can be traveled in an instant. The HEX is a mind ready to transcend the narrow boundaries of the body and become thought without flesh. It takes no trauma to unlock the potential of the HEX. It requires only a mind open to possibilities. Recognize that there are no boundaries and there will be none. <

All over Europe the lights were coming on. Darkened screens burst back into life and filled with data which flowed on and on. Raven's mind weaved itself into the net and the darkness screamed as it dissolved. In the plaza in front of the hotel, Winter the Force Commander and Wraith the Ghost watched as the lights returned to the buildings surrounding them.

In the hotel suite on the seventh floor Kez gasped and the others turned to look at Raven. Her figure was glowing with a strange light. As they watched it brightened until, in the space of moments, it was too blinding to look at. Closing his eyes, Kez reached for her hand and caught it. It felt insubstantial to touch and he clung to it desperately. He could feel the light like an electric current burning through him. It was becoming physically painful to touch Raven. He clung on. But like a building charge the light continued to grow. Even behind his eyelids he could see it and then he could hold on no longer. Colors flashed behind his closed eyes. He could hear a sound building inside his ears: a single note that seemed to come from an infinite distance and yet grew louder all the time. There was no way of describing the sensation although later Ali, who had felt it even in London, described it as like a leap from a high place.

Then abruptly it vanished and he opened his eyes to see that Raven was gone. No trace of her remained. But on the gently glowing screen four words stood out clearly.

> **Let there be light.** <

Epilogue

The world was remade. But not everything changed at once. The dismantling of the old regime took time. Some of the Seccies and the EF troops fought. Others attempted to regain control of the net. Many fled to other countries where Hexes were still illegal and tried to win support for a counter-coup. All of them failed.

However, there were others, like Force Commander Winter, who acknowledged the legitimacy of the new government. It took time to gain their loyalty and many were not accepted as supporters of the Hex government because of crimes they had committed in the past. The new European Communality had to win the faith of its citizens, and many who had been labeled criminals under the old government rose to positions of authority in the new political climate. Even after elections, it took the other world countries more than ten years to recognize the new state. But in the end they caved in.

The European Communality had control
of the network and without its support
the rest of the world was lagging behind in
the race to progress. The achievements of
the Hex government were more than political, they were scientific and technological as
well. Professor Moore, surviving the devastation of the Space Operations Center, lived
for another twenty years, assisted by a
young scientist named Luciel, to see his
dream come true. The much-neglected
space exploration program experienced the
first major change of the new government.
The first President of the European Communality announced in her inaugural
speech that the people of Earth would
spread out to colonize the stars.

"In space our future awaits us," she said.
"It has been waiting for a long time."

The first space ships built by the Communality were captained by Hexes. Later
their names would also become legends:
Gift, Talent and Drow.

In the early years after the revolution
there were many who were surprised that
the new government was not led by a more
prominent figure. The names of the Hexes
who had won freedom for their kind and
for the rest of Europe, and later the world,
had become legends to the citizens of the
Communality. There was a romantic

attraction in the idea of Wraith, the ganger who had risen to high political office. There were others who were fascinated by Avalon, the only Hex who had lived in the public eye and preserved her secret, and could not understand why she declined political responsibility in favor of continuing her career as a musician. The first Communality President came as a surprise to almost everyone, including herself. But electing Allison Marie Tarrell was the wisest choice they could have made. Under her careful governance the new state flourished and expanded.

Her first action as President was to place a monument in the Serendipity district of the city of Transcendence. Later it became legendary itself. Carved from black obsidian, the Raven spread its stone wings for flight, exultation in every feather of its being.

On the first anniversary of the revolution two figures stood by the monument as the celebrations expanded in the city around them.

"I never thought it would end this way," Kez said quietly. "That we'd lose Raven to gain the world."

"Don't think of her as lost," Cloud replied. "She wouldn't have seen it that way."

"How would she have seen it?" Kez asked, as the first stroke of midnight fell and celebrations reached their peak.

"As being the first of us to find her wings," Cloud said, and above them the sky exploded with light.

About the Author

Rhiannon Lassiter is a graduate of Oxford University. The first literary agent to see her work encouraged her to finish *Hex*, which she wrote when she was seventeen, and it was immediately bought by the first publisher who read it. Her mother is a well-known children's author, and she lives in London.

As well as writing, Rhiannon runs her own Web-design business, writes articles and reviews of children's books, and is part of the production team Armadillo, a children's books review publication. Her other interests include computer and role-playing games, watching films, reading, and seeing her friends.